The Uncollected Stories by Edgar Wallace

Volume II

Richard Horatio Edgar Wallace was born on the 1st April 1875 in Greenwich, London. Leaving school at 12 because of truancy, by the age of fifteen he had experience; selling newspapers, as a worker in a rubber factory, as a shoe shop assistant, as a milk delivery boy and as a ship's cook.

By 1894 he was engaged but broke it off to join the Infantry being posted to South Africa. He also changed his name to Edgar Wallace which he took from Lew Wallace, the author of Ben-Hur.

In Cape Town in 1898 he met Rudyard Kipling and was inspired to begin writing. His first collection of ballads, The Mission that Failed! was enough of a success that in 1899 he paid his way out of the armed forces in order to turn to writing full time.

By 1904 he had completed his first thriller, The Four Just Men. Since nobody would publish it he resorted to setting up his own publishing company which he called Tallis Press.

In 1911 his Congolese stories were published in a collection called Sanders of the River, which became a bestseller. He also started his own racing papers, Bibury's and R. E. Walton's Weekly, eventually buying his own racehorses and losing thousands gambling. A life of exceptionally high income was also mirrored with exceptionally large spending and debts.

Wallace now began to take his career as a fiction writer more seriously, signing with Hodder and Stoughton in 1921. He was marketed as the 'King of Thrillers' and they gave him the trademark image of a trilby, a cigarette holder and a yellow Rolls Royce. He was truly prolific, capable not only of producing a 70,000 word novel in three days but of doing three novels in a row in such a manner. It was estimated that by 1928 one in four books being read was written by Wallace, for alongside his famous thrillers he wrote variously in other genres, including science fiction, non-fiction accounts of WWI which amounted to ten volumes and screen plays. Eventually he would reach the remarkable total of 170 novels, 18 stage plays and 957 short stories.

Wallace became chairman of the Press Club which to this day holds an annual Edgar Wallace Award, rewarding 'excellence in writing'.

Diagnosed with diabetes his health deteriorated and he soon entered a coma and died of his condition and double pneumonia on the 7th of February 1932 in North Maple Drive, Beverly Hills. He was buried near his home in England at Chalklands, Bourne End, in Buckinghamshire.

Index of Contents

The Destroyer
The Poisoners
The Four Just Men
Record of Death
The Just Men's Warning

Essley's Secret
Her Birthday
The Despatch Rider
Three War Stories For Children
Chapter I - Sentry No. 1
Chapter II - The Pet of the Wigshires
Chapter III - Frank the Trumpeter
Clarence - Private
Chapter I - The Birth of the Sharpshooters
Chapter II - The Woman of Mons
Chapter III - The Return of the Great Unwanted
Chapter IV - The Losing of Orlando
Chapter V - The Ghost of Napoleon
Chapter VI - The Red Chocolate
Five Fateful Words
Edgar Wallace – A Short Biography
Edgar Wallace – A Concise Bibliography

The Destroyer

Over by Voisney a heliograph made a great trembling splash of light.

"Answer," said the captain, and the corporal tapped the key of the little mirror which stood on a thin-edged tripod before him.

"Le Zallach en vol," he read, and monsieur the captain swore.

"Send back," he said briefly, and a chasseur behind him waved a flag rapidly.

So the news went back to the camp, to the tent before which the tricolour of France flew, to the stout, red-faced man who sat at a table, his head in his hands, studying a map of the country west of Nancy.

The Zallach was flying. The news went like wildfire through the lines. Men sitting in little circles about their tiny fires—it is cold in October in the open country about Nancy—rose and stared blankly and helplessly at the darkening East.

The artillerymen did not rise, for they had only just returned from a hard day's fighting, but they grabbed their food and ate rapidly, knowing that they would he required presently. The 14th Cavalry did not rise because they had been chasing the Zallach for a week, and were sore men, body and soul.

"My friend," said the general to the chief of staff, "my friend, this Zallach is an accursed nuisance!" He was a fat, jolly general, and his tone was one of comical despair.

"In the great war we fought men—men who grovelled and crawled on their stomachs like worms. It was crawl for crawl with us. We saw them creeping through a field and we crept after them; we watched them wriggle round a hill and we wriggled forward to check them. But now we fight birds!"

He shook his head tragically.

On his map, veined blue and red with innumerable lines, were black squares methodically painted. They lay for the main part where blue road-vein and red railway-artery came together in a chaotic ganglion.

"Here," he said, and stuffed his finger upon such a square, "here Madame Zallach destroyed the line, hindering the mobilisation of the 10th Army Corps. Here she came slowly to earth and destroyed the bridge over the Loire, to my embarrassment, and now—"

Contrary to all expectations, no decisive battle had yet been fought between the opposing armies. Since the memorable day when Spain's defeat at El-Malabi had necessitated the occupation of the north of Morocco by French troops, war had been inevitable. It was precipitated by the accidental shelling of the other Power's consulate at El Malabi by a French battery.

But the one decisive battle which military experts demanded to open and close the war had not been waged. Rather the two armies sparred cautiously, making certain preparations. Chief of the instruments of preparation had been the Zallach—officially "his Majesty's airship, Zallach IV."

A great ship this, that could rise and fall at will, go up against a gale or run before it, lower engineers on dark nights to destroy culvert and bridge, and then, before the alarm could be given—whir-r-r! She was up again, her big aluminium nose pointing to the stars, her car canted to an uncomfortable angle, but the men, clutching desperately at her cane rails safe, despite their discomfort.

Twice had the general had her within range, once at dawn, once under his searchlights; but neither field nor aerial artillery came into action as quickly as she went buzzing out of range, a monstrous yellow bee, leaving her sting behind.

"She is not yet in sight, general," reported the chief of staff, but the stout general sat at the table before his map, saying nothing.

"She demoralises the men—she is a nightmare," continued the staff officer; "she is Atropos" (he had a passion for the classics, this chief of staff), "Lachesis, Clotho—"

"And you are Cassandra, the son of the devil," said the general, whose mythology was nil. "Send Monsieur Pelletier to me."

The staff officer saluted and retired.

He came back in a few minutes with a youth who wore a Norfolk suit of unmistakable English cut but whose Parisianism was best displayed in the amplitude of his cravat.

"Monsieur Pelletier," said the general, "I am inclined to risk your valuable life."

The young man smiled cheerfully.

"My friend, Madame Zallach"—the general waved his hand to the door of his tent—"causes me annoyance. Moreover, she is dangerous. She is apparently the only thing that can move over this infernal country by night without falling into a ditch. My artillery cannot reach her, because she knows where the guns are parked and avoids the locality; also she sees us when we take our guns out and goes another way."

The young man bowed again.

"Therefore," said the general more slowly and gravely than was his wont, "I particularly desire that she should be destroyed."

He walked to one end of the tent and took up a small box. It was the size of a tea-chest and fairly light. The lid was fastened with a lock, and this he opened; and, gingerly removing the fine shavings at the top, revealed a curiously-shaped bomb. It was little larger than an orange, but from every part of its surface protruded long, thin hooks and spikes. At one side of the sphere was a light steel staple.

"I have had this made according to your directions, and you will find that it is timed for thirty seconds; you understand, mon vieux?"

"Parfaitement, mon general," said the boy.

"I have decided," the commander went on, "that you shall take with you Monsieur Le Brun."

The youth turned with a stare of blank astonishment.

"But, general," he protested. "Monsieur Le Brun! It is impossible! Monsieur Le Brun! He is a biplane man—we are not agreed—general, you embarrass me."

"Nevertheless," said the general, with a gesture to the world at large, "nevertheless—for the glory of France—besides which," he added thoughtfully, "there is no other aeroplanist in the camp."

The young man drew himself up, bowed, and departed to change. After all, he reflected, it might be worse. But for Le Brun breaking his crankshaft, the task might have been his; and he, Pelletier, might have been obliged to ride a passenger on a preposterous biplane.

"Are you all right?" Pelletier spoke coldly over his shoulder at the man behind him. Le Brun, of the Engineers, himself a famous aeroplanist, was crouching behind him in the boat-like body of the monoplane, and between his knees was the little box no bigger than a small tea-chest.

"All right," he said dubiously; "though, Monsieur Pelletier, you understand that I do not approve of monoplanes; to me, for the ultimate conquest of the air, we must look only to the biplane. Every—"

"I will spare you, monsieur," said the young man with ominous calm, "a lecture on aeronautics, more especially since my own experiments have not been without result."

"In the matter of stability—" began Le Brun.

"Monsieur," said the other, his voice trembling, "you are on the subject most tender to me."

He looked down at the circle of curious soldiers and reached his hand to the general.

"I can just see her," he said, and pointed ahead to where, on the skyline, like a black pencil-mark in the blue-black east, the Zallach hovered.

"Bon voyage, mes braves," said the general, and Pelletier started the motor.

"Hold on!" he said, and six men gripped the light framework of the machine.

"Whir-r-r!" roared the engines, and the thin propeller at the bow whistled round, a blue haze marking its presence.

"Let go!"

The machine leapt forward, running along the level plain at thirty miles an hour, gathering speed as it moved. Pelletier's hands were on the two wheels at his side, his feet on the rudder treads, his eyes fixed ahead.

"Bump, bump, bump!" rushed the monoplane over the uneven ground, then Pelletier cautiously turned his wheels forward, and the two planes at the side of the ship rose obediently. The bumping ceased, there was only a slight swaying from side to side, otherwise the boat seemed to be stationary. Over the side the world was slipping past; the camp was already far behind, and Pelletier pressed the rudder tread and brought the planes back over the camp again.

Twice he circled, ever rising, the camp beneath him growing smaller and smaller till the lines of the bivouacked troops spread beneath him like a gridiron.

"We are now?" he asked, and Le Brun consulted the tiny barometer before him.

"Two hundred metres," he said grudgingly. "Had this been a biplane of the Voison-Farman type, we should—"

"Thank you, monsieur," said Pelletier with elaborate politeness.

"It is very cold," grumbled the man at his back.

"It would be colder on a biplane," said the other, and grinned into the darkness.

Le Brun said nothing; but, after a while, he asked:

"Shall I put out the bomb, m'sieur?"

"Wait until we are clear of the camp, I pray you," said the pilot, and headed the monoplane due north.

All the time the Mignonette was rising, and in the thinner atmosphere she slowed to forty kilometres an hour.

Pelletier was taking a sweep that would bring him up on the blind side of the Zallach. To go flying straight out to the enemy with the afterglow of sunset at his back would be courting calamity. Silhouetted against the evening sky, he would be a fair mark for the riflemen of Madame.

"If monsieur will hang out the bomb," he suggested as the plane cleared the outlying pickets—tiny black dots moving slowly below. Le Brun opened the box, lifted the little black orange carefully, clipped the trailing line to the staple, and lowered it through the bottomless "floor" of the car.

Slowly, slowly, he lowered it, and as slowly Pelletier brought the planes a fraction higher to compensate the disturbed balance.

Le Brun watched the operation with professional interest. He was impressed. He said as much with characteristic generosity.

"I had no idea that a monoplane—" he said; "yet, if you will pardon me, my friend, I should have thought that your great ingenuity would be better employed on a machine of a more—"

"M. Le Brun," said Pelletier, "I am overwhelmed by your praise and appalled by your judgment."

The tiny barometer before Le Brun showed 500 metres, and Pelletier chuckled ruefully.

"This is nearly a record, i>mon ami," he said, "but there is no prix d'altitude for our little Mignonette."

"It is very cold," grumbled Le Brun, evading responsive praise.

Pelletier brought the plane slowly round to the east; all the time he had been watching the faint outlines of the big dirigible, and judged it lo be three miles away, and flying at 300 metres, its favourite height.

It was moving slowly northward at right angles to him, and judging that he had crossed its track he turned southward, so that it would pass him on his right.

He was, he knew, well out of sight, for the monoplane, with its flat surfaces, offered no bulk, and besides, darkness had fallen on the world, save for the pearl-grey glow in the west.

"We are much higher than she," he said. "I hope she is moving."

His only danger lay in the dirigible remaining stationary, for then, with her engines stopped, the whirring of his propeller would be plainly audible. Nearer and nearer the Mignonette crept, and the progress seemed slow though she was moving at thirty miles an hour, and through his night-glasses Le Brun watched.

"She's moving," he said, "and if I'm any judge of perspective we're about 100 metres too high."

Her "deck" was visible now, but it was too dark to see the figures of her crew. Pelletier put his helm over to starboard and brought the Mignonette directly in the track of the balloon, then—

"She's higher than I thought," said Le Brun quickly. "Look! there goes her searchlight—she wouldn't dare use that under four hundred metres."

From the deck shot a long white beam that moved downward. Le Brun saw a little round patch of the green earth appear at the end of the ray, saw the glitter of a thread of river, and a grain of humanity on a white road.

"One of our cavalry outposts," he said. "So long as they keep the light down we are safe."

He glued his glasses to his eyes and watched in silence.

Nearer and nearer swept the little destroyer through the air.

"They've stopped!" whispered Le Brun fiercely; "plane, plane, for God's sake!"

Pelletier's hand went out to shut off the engine. He could plane down to his victim without risk, but he was too late.

The white beam jerked up from its survey of the world below, and began searching the heavens. Left and right, up and down it waved with fierce energy.

"Now!" said Pelletier between his teeth, and dipped his planes. Gathering speed as it slipped down the velvet path of air, the Mignonette came hurtling through space. 200 metres, a hundred, then the searchlight found her, and the white light glared in Pelletier's face. But he was prepared. Swiftly he adjusted the smoked glasses that were on his forehead.

"Zipp—zipp—zizz!"

"Air-guns," muttered Le Brun. "I thought the devils wouldn't risk the rifle at this altitude."

He steadied the swaying bomb that hung between his knees, drew it gently up until it was flush with his foot-rest.

Then the light went out; they were in the upward-cast shadow of the balloon.

"Wait, wait!" screamed Pelletier over his shoulder; "we have overshot them."

"A biplane," muttered Le Brun, "would not have over-shot them."

The mono' tilted alarmingly as it swung round again; the searchlight was thrusting into the darkness in a vain search; it found the monoplane for the second time as it come flying backward to the attack.

"Zip! zip!"

Le Brun felt something slap the side of his head, and shook it like a dog. He felt something warm on his face.

"Now!" yelled Pelletier, and Le Brun slipped a catch and dropped the bomb.

"Zip! zip!"

The searchlight was on them, but the Mignonette was flying at hurricane speed to safety.

Away, away she flow, lower and lower, until looking backward Le Brun saw the big body of the dirigible was above him, and two hundred metres in rear.

"We've failed!" he whispered, and cursed—mainly he cursed human stupidity that put its faith in a boat with wings.

"If it struck the bag it will hold," Pelletier shouted. "We've got about ten more seconds to get out of hell!"

One, two, three!

They were well clear of danger now, for the searchlight had gone out, but there was the risk of wind from the explosion.

"Crash!"

The very heavens seemed to burst into flame and fall; a mighty wind swept the monoplane over to its side, lifted it and threw it through space.

"Hold on!" yelled Pelletier.

Half an hour later he planed down before the general's tent, a white-faced, dishevelled youth, with lines about his eyes.

"Finished," he said sleepily, and tumbled out of his seat like a log. Le Brun descended slowly after him. He seemed to be considering something, then, as Pelletier turned to direct the soldiers who were handling the airship, he said:

"Monsieur, it is due to you to say that nothing but a monoplane could have turned two somersaults in the air, and righted itself at the end. I would add," he said sleepily reflective, "that the biplane would not have turned the somersault, but that is beside the point."

The Poisoners

Called Abroad

Mr. Essley paced up and down his study at Forest Hill. The table was a litter of opened letters, for the doctor was paying one of his brief visits to the practice.

He took up one of the letters and read it again. It was written in French and bore at its head the stamp of the Ministry of Justice. The writer had the honour and felicity to inform M. le Docteur that the Four Just Men had disappeared, as from the face of the earth, and that they were certainly not domiciled in France.

The doctor threw the letter down. They had all said the same. No authority helped him. The new Spanish writer, De la Monte, whose work on crime had recently been translated into English, made no mention of the men. Yet he wrote with assurance, and was a likely man to supply information.

A thought struck him. He turned the leaves of the telephone-book and found a number. He asked for this, and in a few minutes he was speaking with the publisher.

"I am Dr. Essley," he said. "I am most anxious to find the address of the author of a book you have recently published; it is called 'Modern Crime.'"

"De la Monte's?"

"That's the man."

"If you will wait, I will find out," said the voice.

The doctor held on till the speaker returned.

"It is in Cordova."

A sudden light came to Dr. Essley's eyes.

"Yes?" he said eagerly. "Can you give me the exact address?"

"Forty-one Calle Moreria."

"Thank you!" The doctor hastily scribbled the address and hung up the receiver.

Cordova! Of all the providential things in the world! Interest of another kind called him to that city. There was a certain Dr. Cajalos ho wished to see.

He rang the bell, and the old woman who formed the domestic staff of his little house answered it.

"I am going away for a few days," he said. "I have been called to Paris."

"If Mr. Black rings up, sir—"

"He won't ring up," he said shortly; "and, if he does, you may tell him that I am away from town."

Dr. Essley then left the house, walking briskly to the railway-station, very briskly for a grey-haired man, and the vigour of his stride no less than the swing of his shoulders spoke of a strength which is not ordinarily possessed by a man of fifty.

Yet, for all the buoyancy of his walk, he was uncomfortable. He had a hateful suspicion at the back of his mind that he was being watched. Twice he looked round sharply, but saw nothing. Under his breath he cursed his folly.

"I have got these infernal Four Just Men on my nerves," he said to himself.

He reached Victoria and took a taxi-cab to Charing Cross. He had a quarter of an hour to wait. Standing before the bookstall, he had that uncomfortable feeling again. He was being watched. He turned sharply and saw nothing but unoffending passengers. The man who had been watching him had turned a fraction of a second before, and Essley only saw his broad back as he stooped to fasten the strap of his valise.

The doctor, with a bitter little smile of self-disgust, returned to a contemplation of the bookstall. A flaming placard announced the fact that Cresswell Black had gained control of the F. and B. Railway. He bought a paper and read:

"We understand that all obstacles to the amalgamation of the Finsbury and Burset with the North-East London Railway have disappeared with the death of Mr. George Wallison, the late chairman of the F. & B. line. Mr. Wallison, it will be remembered, was taken suddenly ill at a City banquet, and though attended by a doctor, succumbed from heart failure. Mr. Cresswell Black, presiding at a meeting of the N.-E. L. expressed his regret that the realisation of his plans had been made possible by so sad a happening."

Dr. Essley folded the paper under his arm and walked thoughtfully along the platform to his train.

The man who sat at the marble-topped table of the Café de la Gran Capitan, in Cordova, was a man of leisure. A tall man was George Manfred, with a trim beard and grave grey eyes that searched the street absently as though not quite certain of his quest. He sipped a coffee and drummed a little tune on the table with his slender white hands.

He was dressed in black. His cloak was long and lined with black velvet, and the deep collar was faced with the same material. His attire was conventional enough—for Cordova—and, in spite of his grey eyes, he might have been a Spaniard.

His speech was flawless. He spoke with the lisp of Andalusia, clipping his words as do the folk of the South. Also, there was evidence of his Southern origin in his response to the whining beggar who shuffled painfully to him, holding out crooked fingers for largesse.

"In the name of the Virgin, and the Saints, and the God who is above all, I beseech you, senor, to spare me ten centimos."

The bearded man brought his far-seeing eyes to focus on the palm.

"God will provide," he said, in the Arabic-dialect of Spanish Morocco.

"Though I live a hundred years," said the beggar monotonously, "I will never cease to pray for your lordship's happiness."

He of the velvet-lined cloak looked at the beggar.

The mendicant was a man of medium height, sharp-featured, unshaven after the way of his kind, terribly-bandaged across his head, and with one eye. Moreover, he was lame. His feet were shapeless masses of swathed bandages, and his discoloured hands clutched a stick fiercely. "Senor and prince," he whined, "there is between me and the cursed pangs of hunger ten centimos, and your worship would not sleep this night in comfort thinking of me tossing in famine."

The man at the table sipped his coffee unmoved.

"Go with God," he said.

Still the man lingered.

He looked helplessly up and down the sunlit street. He looked into the cool, dark recess of the café, where an apathetic waiter sat at a table reading the "Heraldo." Then he leant forward, stretching out a slow hand to pick a crumb of cake from the next table.

"Do you know Dr. Essley?" he asked in perfect English.

The cavalier at the table looked thoughtful.

"I do not know him. Why?" he asked in the same language.

"You should know him," said the beggar; "he is interesting."

He said no more, shuffling a painful process along the street. The other watched him with some curiosity, then, standing up to his full height—he was well over the six-foot mark—he shook his cloak and began to walk slowly in the direction taken by the beggar.

He overtook the man in the Calle Paraiso, passed him, and finally came to the Bridge of Calahorra. He reached the centre of the bridge and leant over, watching with idle interest the swollen yellow waters of the Guadalquivir.

Out of the corner of his eye he watched the beggar come slowly through the gate in his direction. He had a long time to wait, for the man's progress was slow. At last he came sidling up to him, hat in hand, palm outstretched. The attitude was that of a beggar, but when he spoke the voice was that of an educated Englishman.

"Manfred," he said earnestly, "you must see this man Essley. I have a special reason for asking."

"What is he?"

The beggar smiled.

"I am dependent upon memory to a great extent," he said, "the library at my humble lodgings being somewhat limited; but I have a dim idea that he is a doctor in the suburbs of London; rather a clever surgeon."

"What is he doing here?"

Gonsalez—for such was the beggar's name—smiled again.

"There is in Cordova a Dr. Cajalos. A marvelous man, George, performing miracles undreamt of in your philosophy. Making the blind see, casting spells upon the guilty, and creating infallible love philtres for the innocent."

Manfred nodded.

"I have seen him and consulted him."

The beggar was a little astonished.

"You're a wonderful man, George," he said with admiration in his voice. "When did you do it?"

Manfred laughed softly.

"There was a certain night, not many weeks ago, when a beggar stood outside the worthy doctor's door patiently waiting till a mysterious visitor, cloaked to his nose, had finished his business."

"I remember," said the other, nodding. "He was a stranger from Ronda, and I was curious. Did you see me following him?"

"I saw you," said Manfred gravely. "I saw you from the corner of my eye."

"It was not you?" asked Gonsalez, astonished.

"It was I," said the other. "I went out of Cordova to come into Cordova."

Gonsalez was silent for a moment.

"I accept the humiliation," he said. "Now, since you know the doctor, can you see any reason for the visit of a commonplace English doctor to Cordova? He has come all the way, without a halt, from England by the Algeciras Express. He leaves Cordova to-morrow morning at daybreak by the same urgent system, and he comes to consult Dr. Cajalos."

"Poiccart has written?" asked Manfred.

"Poiccart is here; he has an interest in this Essley. So great an interest that he comes blandly to our Cordova, Baedeker in hand, seeking information of the itinerant guide, and submitting meekly to his inaccuracies."

Manfred stroked his little beard with the same grave thoughtful expression in his wise eyes as when he had watched Gonsalez shuffling from the Café de la Gran Capitan.

"Life would be dull without Poiccart," he said.

"Dull, indeed. Ah, senor, my life shall be your praise, and it shall rise like the smoke of holy incense to the throne of heaven."

He dropped suddenly into his whine, for a policeman of the town guard was approaching with a suspicious eye for the beggar who stood with expectant hand outstretched.

Manfred shook his head as the policeman strolled up.

"Go in peace," he said.

"Dog," said the policeman, his rough hand descending on the beggar's shoulder. "Thief of a thief, begone lest you offend the nostrils of this illustrious."

With arms akimbo, he watched the man limp away, then he turned to Manfred.

"If I had seen this scum before, excellency," he said fiercely, "I should have relieved your presence of his company."

"It is not important," said Manfred conventionally.

The man walked by his side to the end of the bridge, where they stood chatting near the principal entrance to the cathedral.

"Your excellency is not of Cordova?" asked the officer.

"I am of Malaja," said Manfred without hesitation.

"I had a sister who married a fisherman of Malaja," confided the policeman.

Manfred merely nodded. He was interested in a party of tourists who wore being shown the glories of the Puerta del Perdon.

One of the tourists detached himself from the party and came towards them. He was a man of middle height and strongly built. There was a strange reserve in his air, and a saturnine imperturbability in his face.

"Can you direct me to the Passeo de la Gran Capitan?" he asked in bad Spanish.

"I am going that way," said Manfred courteously. "If the senor would condescend to accompany me—"

"I shall be grateful," said the other.

They raised their hats to the policeman—Manfred with ease, the other a little awkwardly—and moved off.

They chatted a little on divers subjects—the weather, the delightful character of the Mosque Cathedral.

"You must come along and see Essley," said the tourist suddenly. He spoke in perfect Spanish.

"Tell me about him," said Manfred. "Between you, my dear Poiccart, you have piqued my curiosity."

"This is an important matter," said the other earnestly. "Essley is a doctor in a suburb of London. I have had him under observation for some months. He has a small practice—quite a little one, and he attends a few cases. Apparently he does no serious work in his suburb, and his history is a strange one.

"He was a student at University College, London, and soon after getting his degree, left with a youth named Black for Australia. Black had been a hopeless failure, and had been badly ploughed in his exams, but the two were fast friends, which may account for their going away together to try their luck in a new country. Neither of them had a relation in the world.

"Arrived in Melbourne, the two started off up-country with some idea of making for the new gold-diggings which were in full swing at that time. I don't know where the diggings were; at any rate, it was three months before Essley arrived—alone, his companion having, it was reported, died on the road. This report could not have been true, for Black eventually turned up after a complete disappearance.

"Essley does not seem to have started practising for three or four years. We can trace his wanderings from mining camp to mining camp, where he dug a little, gambled a lot, and was generally known as Dr. S.—probably an abbreviation of Essley. Not until he reached Western Australia did he attempt to establish himself as a doctor. He had some sort of practice, not a very high-class one, it is true, but certainly lucrative. He disappeared from Coolgardie in 1900. He did not reappear in England until 1908." They had reached the Passeo by now. The streets were better filled than they had been when Manfred had followed the beggar.

"I've some rooms here," said Manfred. "Come in and we will have some tea."

He occupied a flat over a jeweller's in the Calle Moreria. It was a well-furnished apartment, "and especially blessed in the matter of light," explained Manfred as ho inserted the key. He put a silver kettle on the electric stove.

"The table is laid for two?" questioned Poiccart.

"I often have visitors," said Manfred with a little smile. "Sometimes the begging profession becomes an intolerable burden to our Leon, and he enters Cordova by rail, a most respectable member of society, full of a desire for the luxury of life—and stories. Go on with yours, Poiccart; I am interested."

The "tourist" seated himself in a deep armchair.

"Where was I?" he asked. "Oh, yes, Dr. Essley disappeared from Coolgardie, and after an obliteration of eight years he reappeared in London."

"In any exceptional circumstances?"

"No, very ordinarily. He seems to have been taken up by the newest kind of Napoleon—that same companion whose death had been reported, but who was very much alive."

"Cresswell Black?" asked Manfred, raising his eyebrows.

Poiccart nodded.

"The same," he said. "At any rate, Essley, thanks to what practice he could steal from other practitioners in his own suburb—somewhere in the neighbourhood of Forest Hill—and what practice Napoleon's recommendation gives him, seems to be fairly well off. He first attracted my attention—"

There came a tap at the door, and Manfred raised his finger warningly. He crossed the room and opened the door. The concierge stood outside, cap in hand; behind him, and a little way down the stairs, was a stranger—obviously an Englishman.

"A senor to sec your excellency," said the concierge.

"My house is at your disposal," said Manfred, addressing the stranger in Spanish.

"I am afraid I do not speak good Spanish," said the man on the stairs.

"Will you come up?" asked Manfred in English.

The other mounted the stairs slowly.

He was a man of fifty. His hair was grey and long. His eyebrows were thick and shaggy, and his under jaw stuck out and gave his face an appearance which was slightly repulsive. He wore a frock coat and carried a big, soft wide-awake in his gloved hand.

He peered round the room from one to the other.

"My name," he said, "is Essley. Essley," he repeated as though he derived some satisfaction from the repetition—"Dr. Essley." Manfred motioned him to a chair, but he shook his head.

"I'll stand," he said harshly. "When I have business I stand."

He looked suspiciously at Poiccart.

"I have private business," he said pointedly.

"My friend has my complete confidence," said Manfred.

Essley nodded grudgingly.

"I understand," he said, "that you are a scientist and a man with considerable knowledge of Spain."

Manfred shrugged his shoulders. In his present rôle he enjoyed some reputation as a quasi-scientific literateur, and under the name of "De la Monte" had published a book on "Modern Crime."

"Knowing this," said the man, "I came to Cordova, having other business also—but that will keep."

Ho looked round for a chair, and Manfred offered one into which he sank, keeping his back to the window.

"Mr. de la Monte," said the doctor, leaning forward with his hands on his knees and speaking very deliberately, "you have some knowledge of crime."

"I have written a book on the subject," said Manfred, "which is not necessarily the same thing."

"I had that fear," said the other bluntly. "I was also afraid that you might not speak English. Now I want to ask you a plain question, and I want a plain answer."

"So far as I can give you this, I shall be most willing," said Manfred.

The doctor twisted his face nervously, then:

"Have you ever heard of the Four Just Men?" he asked.

There was a little silence.

"Yes," said Manfred calmly, "I have heard of them. Are there not only three now? One was killed, don't you remember?"

"Are they in Spain?"

The question was put sharply.

"I have no exact knowledge," said Manfred. "Why do you ask?"

"Because—" The doctor hesitated. "Oh, well, I am interested. It is said that they unearth villainy that the law does not punish; they—they kill—eh?"

His voice was sharper, his eyelids narrowed till he peered from one to the other through slits.

"Such an organisation is known to exist," said Manfred; "and one knows that they do happen upon unpunished crime—and punish."

"Even to—to killing?"

"They even kill," said Manfred gravely.

"And they go free!" The doctor leapt to his feet with a snarl and flung out his hands in protest. "They go free! All the laws of all nations cannot trap them! A self-appointed tribunal—who are they to judge and condemn? Who gave them the right to sit in judgment? There is a law, and if a man cheats it—"

He checked himself suddenly, shook his shoulders, and sank heavily into the chair again.

"So far as I can secure information upon the subject," he said roughly, "these men are no longer an active force; they are outlawed; there are warrants for them in every country."

Manfred nodded.

"That is very true," he said gently; "but whether they are an active force, time must reveal."

Dr. Essley twisted uncomfortably in his chair. It was evident that the information or assurance he expected to receive from this expert in crime was not entirely satisfactory to him.

"And they are in Spain?" he asked.

"So it is said."

"They are not in France, they are not in Italy, they are not in Russia, nor in Germany," said the doctor resentfully. "They must be in Spain."

He brooded awhile in silence.

"Pardon me," said Poiccart, who had been a silent listener, "but you seem very interested in these men. Would it be offensive to you, if I asked you to satisfy my curiosity as to why you should be anxious to discover their whereabouts?"

"Curiosity also," said the other quickly. "In a sense I am a modest student of crime, as our friend De la Monte is."

"An enthusiastic student," said Manfred quietly.

"I hoped that you would be able to give me some help," said Essley, unmindful of the significant emphasis of the other's tones. "Beyond the fact that they may be in Spain—which, after all, is conjectural—I have learnt nothing."

"They may not even be in Spain," said Manfred, as he accompanied his visitor to the door; "they may not even be in existence; your fears may be entirely groundless."

The doctor whipped round, white to the lips. "Fears?" he said, breathing quickly. "Did you say fears?"

"I am sorry!" laughed Manfred easily. "My English is perhaps not good."

"Why should I fear them?" demanded the doctor aggressively. "Why should I? Your words are chosen very unwisely, sir. I have nothing to fear from the Just Men—or from any other source."

He stood panting in the doorway like a man who is suddenly deprived of breath.

With an effort he collected himself, hesitated a moment, and then, with a stiff little bow, left the room.

He went down the stairs, out to the street, and turned into the Passeo.

There was a beggar at the corner who raised a languid hand.

"Por dios—" he whined.

With an oath Essley struck at the hand with his cane, only to miss it, for the beggar was singularly quick, and, for all the discomforts he was prepared to face, Gonsalez had no desire to endure a hand seamed and wealed; those sensitive hands of his were assets to Gonsalez.

The doctor pursued a savage way to his hotel.

Reaching his room, he locked the door and threw himself into a chair to think. He cursed his own folly; it was madness to have lost his temper even before so insignificant a person as a Spanish dilettante in science.

There was the first half of his mission finished—and it was a failure. He took from the pocket of his overcoat, hanging behind the door, a Spanish Baedeker. He turned the leaves till he came to a map of Cordova. Attached to this was a smaller plan, evidently made by somebody who knew the topography of the place.

He had heard of Dr. Cajalos first from a Spanish anarchist he had met in some of his curious nocturnal prowlings in London. Under the influence of good wine this bold fellow had invested the wizard of Cordova with something approaching miraculous powers: he had also said things which had aroused the doctor's interest to an extraordinary degree. A correspondence had followed; the visit was the result.

Essley looked at his watch. It was nearly seven o'clock. He would dine, then go to his room and change.

He made a hasty toilet in the growing darkness of the room—curiously enough, he did not switch on the light—then he went to dinner.

He had a table to himself, and buried himself in an English magazine he had brought with him. Now and again as he read he would make notes in a little book which lay on the table by the side of his plate. They had no reference to the article he read; they had little association with medical science. On the whole they dealt with certain financial aspects of a certain problem which came into his mind.

He finished his dinner, taking his coffee at the table. Then he rose, put the little notebook in his pocket and the magazine under his arm, and made his way back to his room. He turned on the light, pulled down the blinds, and drew a light dressing-table beneath the lamp. He produced his notebook again, and with the aid of a number of closely-written sheets of paper taken from his valise, he compiled a little table. He was completely engrossed for a couple of hours.

As if some invisible and unheard ala rum clock warned him of his engagement ho closed the book, locked his memoranda in the valise, and struggled into his coat. With a soft felt hat pulled down over his eyes, he left the hotel, and without hesitation took the path which led down to the Calahorra Bridge. The streets through which he passed were deserted, but he had no hesitation, knowing well the lawful character of these unprepossessing little Spanish suburbs.

He plunged into a labyrinth of narrow streets—he had studied his plan to some purpose—and only hesitated when he reached a cul de sac which was more spacious than the street from which it opened. One oil lamp at the farther end added rather to the gloom. Tall windowless houses rose on either side. Each was pierced by a door. On the left door the doctor, after a moment's hesitation, knocked twice.

Instantly it opened noiselessly. He hesitated.

"Enter," said a voice in Spanish. "The senor need not fear."

He stepped into the black void, and the door closed behind him.

"Come this way," said the voice.

In the pitch darkness he could make out the indistinct figure of a little man.

"The lantern went out," said the voice, with a chuckle. "Doubtless blown out by the spirits."

He chuckled again.

"Spirits and devils abound," he said. "In this patch of ground I have spoken with many such. Pleasant enough and obedient, but disconcerting to the stranger. Look"—he stopped suddenly and clutched the other by the arm—"look!" he whispered. "That is the spirit of one who died by poison. He, he!" He giggled horribly, and Essley felt a shiver run down his spine. "A green devil!" the little man went on "and very sad. This is the way of green devils; they do not hop and jump as the others, but drag their feet and sob great tears. Dios!" he muttered. "Why weep they when they died so easily?"

"In God's name do not talk like that!" said Essley hoarsely.

"You must not be disturbed," said the other. They had come to the black bulk of a house, and the doctor heard the fumble of a key in the lock and the snick of it as it turned. "Enter, my friend."

The doctor stepped inside and surreptitiously wiped the sweat from his forehead. The old man lit a lamp, and Essley took stock of him. He was very little; scarcely more than four foot. He had a rough, white beard and head as bald as an egg. His face and hands were both grimy, and his whole appearance bore evidence of his aversion to water.

A pair of black, twinkling eyes were set deep in his head, and the puckering lines about them revealed him as a man who found humour in life. This was Dr. Cajalos, famous man in Spain, though he had no social standing.

The room they were in was vast and high. It was furnished very poorly. On one big table stood an untidy retort, and there were innumerable test-tubes, balances, scales, and graduated measures in various stages of uncleanliness.

"Sit down," said Cajalos. "We will talk quietly, for I have in the next room a senora of high quality to see me, touching a matter of a lost affection."

Essley took the chair offered to him and the doctor seated himself on a high stool by the table. A curious figure he made, with his dangling little legs, his old, old face and his shining bald pate.

"I wrote to you on the subject of certain occult demonstrations," began the doctor, but the old man stopped him with a quick jerk of the hand.

"You came to see me, senor, because of a drug I have prepared," he said—"a preparation of physostymonine."

Essley sprang to his feet.

"I—I did not tell you so," he stammered.

"The green devil told me," said the other seriously. "I have many talks with the foot-draggers, and they speak very truly."

"I thought—"

"Look," said the old man. He leapt down from his high perch with agility. In the dark corner of one of the rooms were some boxes to which he went. Essley heard a scuffling, and by-and-by the old man came back holding by the ears a wriggling rabbit.

With his disengaged hand he unstoppered a little green bottle on the table. Ho picked a feather from the table, dipped the point gingerly into the bottle. Then very carefully he lightly touched the nose of the rabbit with the end of the feather, so lightly indeed that the feather hardly brushed the muzzle of the animal. Instantly, with no struggle, the rabbit went as limp as though the life essence had been withdrawn from the body. Cajalos replaced the stopper and thrust the feather into a little charcoal fire that burnt dully in the centre of the room.

"Physostymonine," he said briefly; "but my preparation."

He laid the dead animal on the floor at the feet of the other.

"Senor," he said proudly, "you shall take that animal and examine it; you shall submit it to tests beyond patience. Yet you shall not discover the alkaloid that killed it."

"That is not so," said Essley, "for there will be a contraction of the pupil, which is an invariable sign."

"Search also for that," said the old man triumphantly.

Essley made the superficial tests. There was not oven this invariable sign.

A dark figure pressed close to the wall outside, listening. He was standing by the shuttered window. He held to his ear a little ebonite tube with a microphonic receiver, and the rubber which covered the bell-like end was pressed against the shutter.

For half an hour he stood thus, almost motionless, then he withdrew silently and disappeared into the shadows of the orange grove that grew in the centre of the long garden.

As he did so the floor of the house opened, and, with lantern in hand, Cajalos showed his visitor into the street.

"The devils are greener than ever," chuckled the old man. "Hey, there will be happenings, my brother!"

Essley said nothing. He wanted to be in the street again. He stood quivering with nervous impatience as the old man unfastened the heavy door, and when it swung open, he almost leapt into the street outside.

"Good-bye!" he said.

"Go with God," said the old man, and the floor closed noiselessly.

Record of Death

Cresswell Black was a name to conjure with in certain circles. In others it was never mentioned. The financial lords of the City, the Farings, the Wertheimers, the Scott Teasons, had no official knowledge of his existence.

They read of Cresswell Black in their grave way, because there were days when he dominated the financial columns. They read of his mighty stock deals, of his Argentine electric deal, his rubber flotations, and his Canadian copper mines. They read about him, neither approving nor disapproving. They regarded him with the dispassionate interest that a railway engine has for a motorcar.

Black came to the City of London one afternoon to attend a board of directors' meeting. He had been out of town for a few days, recruiting in advance, as he informed the board with a touch of facetiousness, for the struggle that awaited him.

He was a man of middle height, broad of shoulder. His face was thin and lank, his complexion sallow, with a curious uniform yellowness. If you saw Cresswell Black once you would never forget him. Not only because of that yellow face of his, that straight black bar of eyebrow and the thin-lipped mouth, but the very personality of the man impressed itself indelibly on the mind of the observer

His manner was quick, almost abrupt; his replies brusque. A sense of finality marked his decisions. If the financial lords knew him not, there were thousands that did. His name was a household word in England. There was hardly a middle-class family that did not hold his stock. The little "street punters" hung on his word; his issues were subscribed for twice over. And he had established himself in five years. Unknown before that time, he had risen to the dizziest heights in that short space of time.

Punctual to the minute, he entered the board room of the suite of offices he occupied in Moorgate Street.

The meeting had threatened lo be a stormy one. Again an amalgamation was in the air, and again the head of one group of ironmasters—it was an iron combine he was forming—had stood against the threats and blandishments of Black and emissaries.

"The others are weakening," said Fanks. "You promised us that you would put Sandford straight."

"I will keep my promise," said Black shortly.

"Widdison stood out, but he died," continued Fanks. "We can't expect Providence to help us all the time."

Black's eyebrows lowered.

"I do not like jests of that kind," he said. "Sandford is an obstinate man, a proud man; he needs delicate handling. Leave him to me."

The meeting adjourned lamely enough, and Black was leaving the room when Fanks beckoned to him.

"By the way," he said. "I met a man yesterday who knew your friend, Dr. Essley, in Australia."

"Indeed?"

Cresswell Black's face was expressionless.

"Yes, he knew him in his very early days. He was asking me where he could find him."

The other shrugged his shoulders.

"Essley is abroad, I think. You don't like him?"

Augustus Fanks shook his head.

"I don't like doctors who come to see me in the middle of the night, who are never to be found when they are wanted, and are always jaunting off to the Continent."

"He is a busy man," excused Black. "By the way, where is your friend staying?"

"It isn't a friend—he's a sort of prospector, name of Weld, who has come to London with a mining proposition. He is staying at Verlet's Temperance Hotel in Bloomsbury."

"I will tell Essley when he returns," said Black, nodding his head.

He returned to his private office in a thoughtful mood. All was not well with Cresswell Black. Reputed a millionaire, he was in the position of many a financier who counts his wealth in paper. He had got so far, climbing on the shadows. The substance was still beyond his reach. He had organised successful organisations, but the cost had been heavy. Millions had flowed through his hand, but precious little had stuck.

He was in the midst of an unpleasant reverie when a tap on the door aroused him. It opened to admit Fanks.

He frowned at the intruder, but the other pulled up a chair and sat down.

"Look here, Black," he said. "I want to say something to you."

"Say it quickly."

Fanks took a cigar from his pocket and lit it.

"You've had a marvellous career," he said. "I remember when you started with a little bucket-shop in Copthall House—well, we won't call it a bucket-shop," he said hastily as he saw the anger rising in Black's face—"outside-broker's. You had a mug—I mean, an inexperienced partner who found the money."

"Yes."

"He died unexpectedly, didn't he?"

"I believe he did," said Black abruptly.

"Providence again," said Fanks slowly. "Then you got the whole of the business. You took over the flotation of a rubber company, and it panned out. Well, after that you floated a tin mine or something. There was a death there, wasn't there?"

"I believe there was—one of the directors. I forget his name."

Fanks nodded.

"He could have stopped the flotation; he was threatening to resign and expose some methods of yours."

"He was a very headstrong man."

"And he died."

"Yes"—a pause—"he died."

Fanks looked at the man who sat opposite to him.

"Dr. Essley attended him."

"I believe he did."

"Yet still he died."

Black leant over the desk.

"What do you mean?" he asked.

"Nothing; except that Providence has been of some assistance to you," said Fanks. "The record of your success is a record of death; you sent Essley to see me once."

"You were ill."

"I was," said Fanks grimly, "and I was also troubling you a little." He flicked the ash from his cigar to the carpet. "Black, I'm going to resign all my directorships on your companies."

The other man laughed unpleasantly.

"You can laugh; but it isn't healthy, Black. I've no use for money that is bought at too heavy a price."

"My dear man, you can resign," said Cresswell Black; "but might I ask if your extraordinary suspicions are shared by anybody else?"

Fanks shook his head.

"Not at present," ho said.

They looked at one another for the space of half a minute.

"I want to clear right out," Fanks continued. "I reckon my holdings are worth £150,000. You can buy them."

"You amaze me," said Black harshly.

He opened a drawer of his desk and took out a little green bottle and a feather.

"Poor Essley," he smiled, "wandering about Spain seeking the secrets of Moorish perfumery. He would go off his head if he knew what you thought of him."

"I'd sooner he went off his head than that I should go off the earth," said Fanks stolidly. "What have you got there?"

Black unstoppered the bottle and dipped in the feather.

He withdrew it and held it close to his nose.

"What is it?" asked Fanks curiously.

For answer Black held up the feather for the man to smell.

"I can smell nothing," said Fanks.

Tilting the tip quickly downwards, Black drew it across the lips of the other.

"Here—" cried Fanks, and went limply to the ground.

Dr. Essley was in his study, making a very careful microscopic examination. The room was in darkness, save for the light which came from a powerful electric lamp directed on to the reflector of the instrument. What he found on the slide was evidently satisfactory, for by and by he removed the strip of glass, threw it into the fire, and turned on the lights.

He took up a paper from the table and read it.

One item of news interested him. It was an account of the sudden death of Mr. Augustus Fanks, a well-known company director.

"The deceased gentleman," read the account, "was engaged with Mr. Cresswell Black, the famous financier, discussing the details of the new Iron Amalgamation, when he suddenly collapsed, and before medical assistance could be procured, expired. Death was due, it is believed, to heart failure."

There would be no inquest, as Essley knew, for Fanks had, in truth, a weak heart, and had been under the care of a specialist, who, since his speciality was heart trouble, discovered symptoms of the disease on the slightest pretext.

So that was the end of Fanks. The doctor nodded slowly. Yes, that was the end of him. And now?

He took a letter from his pocket. It was addressed to him in the round, sprawling calligraphy of Sandford.

Essley had met him in the early days when Sandford was on friendly terms with Black, he had been recommended to the ironmaster by the financier, and had treated him for divers ills whenever the northerner had come to London. "My London doctor," old Sandford had called him. The ironmaster was staying in London and had written to him.

"Though I am not seeing eye to eye with our friend Black," he wrote, "and we are for the moment at daggers drawn, I trust that this will not affect our relationships, the more so since I wish you to see my daughter who is staying with me."

Edith Sandford was the apple of the old man's eye. Essley remembered having seen her once—a tall girl, with eyes that danced with laughter and a complexion of milk and roses.

He put the letter in his pocket, went into his little surgery, and locked the door. When he came out he wore his long overcoat and carried a little satchel. He had just time to catch a train for the City, and at eleven o'clock he found himself in the ironmaster's private sitting-room at the Grand South Central Hotel.

"You are a weird man, doctor," said the ironmaster with a smile, as he greeted his visitor. "Do you visit most of your patients by night?"

"My aristocratic patients," said the other coolly.

"A bad job about poor Fanks," said the ironmaster. "He and I were only dining together the other night. Did he tell you that he met a man who know you in Australia?"

A shadow of annoyance passed over the other's face.

"Let us talk about your daughter," he said brusquely. "What is the matter with her?"

The ironmaster smiled sheepishly.

"Nothing, I hope. Yet you know, Essley, she is my only child, and I sometimes imagine she is looking ill. My doctor in Newcastle tells me that there is nothing wrong with her."

"I see," said Essley. "Where is she?"

"She is at the theatre," confessed the father. "You must think I am an awful fool to bring you up to town to discuss the health of a girl who is at the theatre."

"Most fathers are fools," said the other. "I will wait till she comes in." He strolled to the window and looked out on the brilliantly illuminated street.

"Why have you quarrelled with Black?" he asked suddenly.

The older man frowned.

"Business," he said shortly. "He is pushing me into a corner. I helped him four years ago—"

"He helped you, too," interrupted the doctor.

"But not so much as I helped him," said the other obstinately. "I gave him his chance. He floated my company, and I profited, but he profited more. The business has now grown to such vast proportions that it will not pay me to come in. Nothing will alter my determination."

"I see," Essley whistled a little tune as he walked again to the window.

Such a man as this must be broken, he thought. Broken! And there was only one way. That daughter of his. He could do nothing to-night. That was evident—nothing.

"I do not think I will wait for your daughter," he said. "Perhaps I will call in to-morrow evening."

"I am so sorry—"

But the doctor silenced him.

"There is no need to be sorry," he said with acerbity. "You will find my visit charged for in my bill."

The ironmaster laughed as he saw him to the door.

"You are almost as good a financier as your friend," he said.

"Almost." said the doctor dryly.

The Just Men's Warning

Essley went straight to the nearest call-office and rang up a temperance hotel in Bloomsbury.

He had reasons for wishing to meet that Mr. Weld who knew him in Australia.

He had no difficulty in getting the message through. Mr. Weld was in the hotel. He waited whilst the attendant found him. By and by a voice spoke.

"I am Weld. Do you want me?"

"Yes, my name is Cole. I knew you in Australia. I have a message for you from a mutual friend. Can you see me to-night?"

"Yes, where?"

Dr. Essley had already decided the place of meeting.

"Outside the main entrance of the British Museum," he said. "There are few people about there at this time of night, and I am less likely to miss you."

There was a pause at the other end of the wire.

"Very good," said the voice. "In a quarter of an hour?"

"That will suit me admirably. Good-bye!"

He hung up the receiver. Leaving his satchel at the cloak-room at Charing Cross Station, he set out to walk to Great Russell Street. He would take no cab. There should be no evidence of that description. Black would not like it. He smiled at the thought.

Great Russell Street was deserted save for a constant stream of taxi-cabs passing and repassing, and an occasional pedestrian. He found his man waiting. Rather tall, and slight, with an intellectual, refined face.

"Dr. Essley?" he asked, coming forward as the other halted.

"My name is Cole," Essley said harshly. "What made you think I was Essley?"

"Your voice," said the other calmly. "After all, it does not matter what you call yourself. I want to see you."

"And I you," said Essley. They walked along side by side until they came to a side street.

"What do you want of me?" asked the doctor.

The other laughed.

"I wanted to see you—you are not a bit like the Essley I knew. He was slighter and had not your colouring, and I was always under the impression that the Essley who went up into the bush died."

"It is possible," said Essley in an absent way. He wanted to gain time. The street was empty. A little way down there was a gateway in which a man might lie unobserved until a policeman came.

In his pocket he had an impregnated feather carefully wrapped up in lint and oiled silk. He drew it from his pocket furtively, and, with his hands behind him, he stripped it of its covering.

"In fact. Dr. Essley," the man was saying, "I am under the impression that you are an impostor."

Essley faced him.

"You think too much," he said in a low voice, "and, after all, I do not recognise you. Turn your face to the light."

The young man obeyed. It was the moment. Quick as thought Essley raised the feather.

A hand of steel gripped his wrist. As if from the ground two other men had appeared. Something soft was thrust into his face. A sickly aroma overpowered him. He struggled madly, but the odds were too many, and then a shrill police-whistle sounded, and he dropped to the ground.

He awoke to find a policeman bending over him. Instinctively he put his hand to his head.

"Hurt, sir?" asked the man.

"No."

He struggled to his feet and stood unsteadily.

"Did you capture the men?"

"No, sir; they got away. I just spotted them as they downed you, but, bless your heart, they seemed to be swallowed up by the earth."

Essley looked around for the feather. It had disappeared. With some reluctance he gave his name and address to the constable, who called a taxi-cab.

"You're sure you've lost nothing, sir?" asked the man.

"Nothing," said Essley testily. "Nothing. Look here, constable, do not report this." He slipped a sovereign into the man's hand. "I do not wish this matter to get into the papers."

"Very good, sir," said the man, "but I shall have to mention it. You see, I blew my whistle, and my mate will report it even if I didn't."

With that Essley had to be content. He drove home to Forest Hill, thinking, thinking.

Who were these three? What object had they?

He was no nearer the solution when he reached his home. He unlocked the door and let himself in. There was nobody in the house but himself and the old woman upstairs.

His comings and goings were so erratic that he had organised a system which allowed him the most perfect freedom of movement.

There must be an end to Dr. Essley, he decided. Essley must disappear from London. He need not warn Black—Black would know.

He would settle the business of the ironmaster and his daughter, and then—there would be a finish.

He unlocked his study, entered, and switched on the lights.

There was a letter on his writing-table, a letter enclosed in a thin grey envelope. He picked it up and examined it. It had been delivered by a messenger, and bore his name, written in a firm hand.

He looked at the writing-table and started back.

The letter had been written in the room and blotted on the pad!

There was no doubt at all about it. The blotting-paper had been placed there fresh that day, and the reverse of the bold handwriting on the envelope was plain to see.

He looked at the envelope again.

It could not have been a patient; he had none. The practice was a blind. Besides, the door had been locked and he alone had the key. He tore the envelope open and took out the contents. It was a half-sheet of note-paper. The three lines of writing ran:

You escaped to-night and have only forty-eight hours
to prepare yourself for the fate which awaits you.
The Just Men.

He sank into his chair, crushed by the knowledge.

They were the Just Men—and he had escaped them.

The Just Men! He buried his face in his hands and tried to think. Forty-eight hours they gave him. Much could be done in forty-eight hours. The terror of death was upon him who had, without qualm or remorse, sent so many on the long journey.

He clutched at his throat and glared round the room. Essley the poisoner—the expert, a specialist in death. The man who had revived the lost art of the Medicis, and had hoodwinked the law. Forty-eight hours. Well, he could settle the business of the ironmaster. That was necessary to Black.

He began to make feverish preparations for the future. There were no papers to destroy. He went into the surgery and emptied three bottles down the sink. The fourth he would want. The fourth had been useful to Black. A little green bottle with a glass stopper. He slipped it into his pocket.

He let the tap run to wash away all trace of the drug he had spilt. The bottles he smashed and threw into a waste bin.

He went upstairs to his room, but he could not sleep. He locked his door and put a chair against it. With a revolver in his hand, he searched the cupboard and beneath the bed. He placed the revolver under his pillow and tried to sleep.

Next morning found him haggard and ill, but none the less he made his toilet with customary care.

Punctually at noon he presented himself at the ironmaster's hotel, and was shown into the sitting-room.

The girl was alone when he entered. He noted with approval that she was very beautiful. That Edith Sandford did not like him, he knew by instinct. He saw the cloud come to her pretty face as he came into her presence, and was amused in his cold way.

"My father is out," she said.

"That is good," said Essley, "for now we can talk."

He seated himself without invitation.

"I think it is only right to tell you, Dr. Essley, that my father's fears regarding me are quite groundless."

At that moment the ironmaster came in and shook hands warmly with the doctor.

"Well, how do you think she looks?" he asked.

"Looks tell you nothing," said the other. It was not the moment for the feather. He had other things to do, and the feather was not the way. He chatted with the two for a while, and then rose. "I will send you some medicine," he said as he rose,

She pulled a wry face.

"Can you come to dinner?" asked Sandford.

Essley considered. That would give him a chance.

"Yes," he said, "I will come."

He took a cab to some chambers near the Thames Embankment, He had a most useful room there.

Mr. Sandford had an appointment with Cresswell Black. It was the final interview before the break.

The City was busy with rumours. A whisper had gone the rounds—all was not well with the financier; the amalgamation on which so much depended had not gone through.

Black sat at his desk that afternoon, twiddling a paper-knife. He was more sallow than usual; the hand that held the knife twitched nervously.

"Essley will have to go," he muttered. "He is too dangerous—far too dangerous. He has outlived his usefulness, and a man who outlives his usefulness is already dead."

He looked at his watch. It was time Sandford came. He pushed a bell by the side of his desk, and a clerk appeared.

"Has Mr. Sandford arrived?" he asked.

"He has just come in, sir," said the man.

"Show him in."

The two men exchanged formal greetings, and Black pointed to a chair.

"Sit down, Sandford," he said curtly. "Now exactly how do we stand?"

"Where we did," said the ironmaster uncompromisingly.

"You will not come into my scheme?"

"I will not," said the other.

Mr. Cresswell Black tapped the desk with his knife, and Sandford looked at him. He seemed older than when Sandford had last seen him. His yellow face was seamed and lined.

"It means ruin for me," he said suddenly. "I have more creditors than I can count. If the amalgamation went through I should be established."

"That is your fault," said the other. "You have taken on too big a job—more than that, you have taken too much for granted."

The man at the desk looked up from under his straight brows.

"It is all very well for you to sit there and tell me what I should do," he said, and the shakiness of his voice told the other something of the passion he concealed. "I do not want advice or homily—I want money. Come into my scheme and amalgamate, or—"

"Or?" repeated the ironmaster defiantly. "Do you think I am afraid of threats?"

"I do not threaten you," said Black sullenly. "I warn you—you are risking more than you know."

"I'll take the risk," said Sandford. He got up on his feet. "Have you anything more to say?"

"Nothing."

"Then I'll bid you good-bye."

The door closed with a slam behind him, and Black leapt up, his face working convulsively.

"Essley shall do his best job!" he vowed.

There was no more work for him to do. He drove back to the handsome flat he occupied in Victoria Street and let himself in.

"There is a gentleman waiting to see you, sir," said his man, who came hurrying to help him out of his coat.

"What sort of a man?"

"I don't know exactly, sir, but I have got a feeling that he is a detective."

"A detective?"

He found his hands trembling and cursed his folly. He stood uncertainly in the centre of the hall. In a minute he had mastered his fears and turned the handle of the door.

A man rose to meet him.

He had a feeling that he had met him before. It was one of those impressions it is so difficult to explain.

"You wanted to see me?" he asked.

"Yes, sir," said the man, a note of deference in his voice. "I have called to make a few inquiries."

It was on the tip of Black's tongue to ask him whether he was a police-officer, but somehow he had not the courage to frame the words.

The effort was unnecessary, as it proved, for the next words of the man explained his errand.

"I have been engaged," he said, "by a firm of solicitors to discover the whereabouts of Dr. Essley."

Black looked hard at him.

"There ought to be no difficulty," he said, "in that. The doctor's name is in the directory."

"That is so," said the man, "and yet I have had the greatest difficulty in running him to earth. As a matter of fact," explained the man, "I was wrong when I said I wanted to discover his whereabouts. It is his identity I wish to establish."

"I do not follow you," said Black.

"Well," said the man, "I don't know exactly how to put it. If you know Dr. Essley, you will recall the fact that he was for some years in Australia?"

"That is true," said Black. "He and I went out together."

"And you were there some years, sir?"

"Yes, we were there for a number of years, though we were not together all the time."

"I see," said the man. "You came home together, I believe?"

"No," replied the other sharply. "We came at different periods."

"Have you seen him recently?"

"No. I have never seen him, although I have frequently written to him on various matters." Black was trying hard not to lose his patience. It would not do for this man to see how much the questions were irritating him.

The man jotted down something in his notebook, closed it, and put it in his pocket.

"Would you be surprised to learn," he asked quietly, "that the real Dr. Essley who went out with you to Australia died there?"

Black's fingers caught the edge of the table, and he steadied himself.

"I did not know that," he said. "Is that all you have to ask?"

"I think that will do, sir," said the detective.

"Can I ask you on whose behalf you are inquiring?" demanded Black.

"That I am not at liberty to tell."

After the detective had gone, Black paced the apartment deep in thought. Assuredly Essley must go.

He took down from the shelf a Continental Baedeker and worked out with a pencil and paper a line of retirement. It might well be that Cresswell Black would have to go, too. If so, it was best to be prepared. His game was up. The refusal of Sandford to negotiate with him was the crowning calamity.

He crossed the room to the safe which stood in the corner, and opened it. In the inside drawer were three flat packets of notes. He picked them out and laid them on the table. They were notes of the Bank of France, each tor a thousand francs.

It would be well to take no risks. He put them in the inside pocket of his coat. If all things failed, they were the way to freedom.

As for Essley—he smiled. He must go, anyway.

He left his flat and drove eastwards to the city.

And as he went, two men followed him, unseen.

Essley's Secret

It was a gay little party that assembled at the Great South Central Hotel. Edith Sandford had invited a girl friend, and Mr. Sandford had brought back the junior partner of one of the City houses he did business with.

Essley was in his workaday clothes, but that did not occasion any surprise, because he had never been known to wear the conventional garb of the Englishman-at-dinner.

He was obviously ill-at-ease and nervous. The second warning of the Just Men had arrived that evening as mysteriously as had the first.

"Sit down, Essley," said Sandford.

There was a vacant chair between the ironmaster and his daughter, and into this the doctor dropped.

His hand shook as he took up his soup-spoon.

He put the spoon down again and unfolded his serviette.

A letter dropped out. He knew those grey envelopes now, and, crushed the letter into his pocket without attempting to read it.

From then on, that letter in his pocket obsessed his every thought. A letter that he touched secretly from time to time to make certain that it was still there. One half of his brain was engaged in this occupation, the other half concerned itself with a glass. It was a bright wineglass on his left and on the girl's right. She would drink champagne from this later. That was an important matter. She would drink champagne from it, and go sliding to the floor like a marionette figure when the strings were cut. If he could—but he was losing his nerve.

A week ago there would have been no difficulty; he would have taken the bold step. Now he feared. Every movement, he felt, was watched. That was the awfulness of it. Any one of these suave waiters, moving silently from guest to guest, might be one of the Just Men. Once he stretched out his hand to take her glass. Then he had the consciousness that every eye was fixed on him.

It was nearly time; he saw one of the waiters twisting the wires from the champagne bottles. The table was in a roar at some sally made by the junior partner. The waiters were hovering about the man with the bottle.

In a second the bottle of green fluid was on Essley's lap—uncorked. He spilt a little on the corner of his serviette, re-stoppered the bottle, and slipped it into his pocket. He took the glass on to his lap. Twice he wiped the drinking edge of it with the damp napkin. He replaced the glass unnoticed.

Now it was done, he felt better. He leant back in his chair, his hands thrust deep into his trousers' pockets. It was an inelegant attitude, but he derived a sense of comfort.

"Essley! Wake up, my dear fellow!" Sandford was talking to him, and he roused himself with a start. "My friend here was rude enough to comment on your hair."

"Eh?" Essley put his hand to his head.

"Oh, it's all right, and it isn't disarranged; but you're a fairly young man to have white hair."

"Yes."

He did not further the discussion.

The waiter filled the glasses. First, the girl's, then his.

He raised his own with unconcern and drank it off. He saw the young girl's slim white fingers close round the stem of the glass, saw her half-raise it, still looking to her partner.

Essley pushed his chair a little to one side as the glass reached her lips. She drank, not much, but enough.

The doctor held his breath. She replaced the glass, still talking with the matron her left.

Essley counted the slow seconds, he counted sixty—a hundred, oblivious to the fact that Sandford was talking to him.

The drug had failed!

The doctor searched furtively in his pocket. He found the bottle again. With, a finger he removed the stopper and brought it out.

"What is that over there?" he asked suddenly. Every eye was directed to the corner of the room to which he pointed. Quickly he emptied the contents into the girl's glass.

"I see nothing. What is it?" asked Sandford.

"Nothing—nothing, I am afraid I have been overworking."

In two minutes he was normal. Laughing awkwardly over his own folly, he refused, to leave.

Again he watched and waited, but this time he took part in the conversation. Somebody proposed the health of the host. It was a jesting toast, but every glass went up. The girl's with the rest.

Nothing happened.

Two minutes went past. The drug could not have lost its potency. He put his hand into his pocket and touched the letter. He took it out:

"Excuse me," he said gruffly as he tore open the letter; "I forgot to read this."

He took out a half-sheet of notepaper.

He smoothed it carefully and read it.

"You will save yourself trouble if you know that we have replaced the poison of Dr. Cajalos with water.

"The Just Men."

He left the table hurriedly and went blundering blindly from the room.

In the corridor of the hotel he came in his haste into collision with a man. It was the man who had called upon Black that afternoon.

NOTE. Two versions of the ending were printed. The first is as printed in The Thriller magazine

"Excuse me," said the man, catching his arm, "I am Detective-sergeant Kay from Scotland Yard, and shall take you into custody."

At the first hint of danger the doctor drew back. Suddenly his fist shot out and caught the officer under the jaw. It was a terrific blow, and the detective was unprepared. He went down like a log.

The corridor was empty. Leaving the man upon the floor, the fugitive sped into the lobby. He was hatless, but he shaded his face with his hand, and passed through the throng in the vestibule into the open air. He signalled a taxi.

"To New Cross Station," he said.

He dismissed the driver at the station, and took a ticket to London Bridge. The train came in as he reached the platform. He found an empty first-class carriage and entered it.

As the train moved out a man came racing down the stairs. He leapt on the footboard as the train moved.

In his carriage Essley went rapidly to work. He pulled down the blinds. It was by great good fortune a main line train. There was washing apparatus in the lavatory. He went to work rapidly.

He had finished before the train came to London Bridge. He pulled the blinds up; came face to face with a man standing on the footboard—a man with stern, grave eyes.

"De la Monte!" he shrieked, and aimed a savage blow at the other.

It never reached him. De la Monte had slipped along the footboard into the open door of a carriage. Essley pulled up the window again and drew down the blind. He took a revolver from his pocket and looked at it stupidly.

On the platform a group of officers waited.

"I had a telephone message," explained a panting officer, "telling me our man was on this train."

"Have they arrested the other man yet?" asked the inspector.

"Black? No, sir. We have got men in his flat waiting for him. I wonder who sent the telephone message?"

The train came to a standstill, and the little group began their search. One window had the blind down. They opened the door.

On the floor lay a man, a revolver by his side.

"That's queer," said the inspector, looking at the dead man's face. "So that was Essley's secret!"

A colleague looked up sharply.

"This man isn't Essley," he snapped.

"I'm afraid you're wrong," answered the inspector. "It's Essley—and Cresswell Black as well. They're one and the same man!"

The second is as printed in The Just Men of Cordova

"I am Detective-Sergeant Kay from Scotland Yard, and shall take you into custody."

At the first hint of danger the colonel drew back. Suddenly his fist shot out and caught the officer under the jaw. It was a terrific blow and the detective was unprepared. He went down like a log.

The corridor was empty. Leaving the man upon the floor, the fugitive sped into the lobby. He was hatless, but he shaded his face and passed through the throng in the vestibule into the open air. He signalled a taxi. "Waterloo, and I will give you a pound if you catch my train."

He was speeding down the Strand in less than a minute. He changed his instructions before the station was reached.

"I have lost the train—drop me at the corner of Eaton Square."

At Eaton Square he paid the cabman and dismissed him. With little difficulty he found two closed cars that waited.

"I am Colonel Black," he said, and the first chauffeur touched his cap. "Take the straightest road to Southampton and let the second man follow behind." The car had not gone far before he changed his mind. "Go first to the Junior Turf Club in Pall Mall," he said.

Arrived at the club, he beckoned the porter. "Tell Sir Isaac Tramber that he is wanted at once," he directed.

Ikey was in the club—it was a chance shot of the colonel's, but it bagged his man.

"Get your coat and hat," said Black hurriedly to the flustered baronet.

"But—"

"No buts," snarled the other savagely. "Get your coat and hat, unless you want to be hauled out of your club to the nearest police-station."

Reluctantly Ikey went back to the club and returned in a few seconds struggling into his great-coat. "Now what the devil is this all about?" he demanded peevishly; then, as the light of a street lamp caught the colonel's uncovered head, he gasped: "Good Lord! Your hair has gone white! You look just like that fellow Essley!"

Her Birthday

Redwood, of the firm of Redwood & Fenner, came into the office in evening dress, for he was dining with Sigley that night. Much depended on the interview. Sigley would be the principal creditor if things went wrong, and things were going as wrong as they could. He was nervous. That he had dressed an hour before dressing was necessary was proof enough of his jumpiness.

Margaret Marsden was cool enough. The sight of her busy fingers manipulating the keys of the typewriter soothed him; the click-click of the machine was an admirable sedative.

Redwood strolled aimlessly down to his desk, stared thoughtfully at the pad, and dropped his overcoat over the back of a chair. The buzzer on the desk sounded. He picked up the receiver—it communicated with the hall-porter's box.

"Yes? Detective-Inspector Harrod from the Criminal Investigation Department?" His eyes narrowed.

"Detective Inspector Harrod?" he repeated thoughtfully. "Tell him to come up."

The hand that pulled open the drawer of the desk shook a little. He had been more reckless in his transactions than a member of an established firm of Hatton Garden jewel merchants should have been. He took a revolver from the drawer of his desk and examined it with a speculative eye. Then he replaced it and closed the drawer.

"Miss Marsden," he said.

The girl looked round.

"Yes, Mr. Redwood."

He was caressing his little black moustache meditatively.

"My bag is in the next room," he said after a moment's hesitation. "It is rather heavy, but I may want you to take it to Charing Cross cloakroom—if necessary. It may not be necessary, but if I have to—to go out, wait until I am gone, then get the bag away."

"I see," said the girl, and looked at him strangely.

There was a knock at the door, and the florid Detective-Inspector entered.

"Good evening, Inspector," Redwood nodded, keeping his eyes fixed on the other's face. The man smiled, so it was all right, thought Redwood. Sigley had not discovered that his diamonds had been pledged.

"I am lucky to catch you here," said the Inspector.

"Catch me?"

Inspector Harrod laughed.

"That's an unfortunate term for a detective to use, isn't It?" he chuckled.

He sat down at the other's invitation, but refused the proffered cigarette.

Redwood was terribly nervous. It required all his effort of will to disguise his apprehension.

"You're going out?" said the detective, seeing the other's attire. "I won't keep you long."

"My time is yours," answered Redwood.

The detective leant over the desk and began in his businesslike way:

"Now, sir, it has come to our knowledge that you have—" He looked round. "Can I speak before your stenographer?" he asked, lowering his voice.

Redwood nodded.

"Yes. She—er—she is in my confidence. I mean in our confidence," he corrected himself hastily.

Harrod nodded.

"Very good. It has come to our knowledge that you have in your office safe pearls to the value of £20,000."

Redwood agreed with an inclination of his head.

"Yes, the Lai Singh rope."

"A remarkable set?" suggested the officer.

Redwood shrugged his shoulders.

"Not remarkable save for the quantity; they are just a number of perfect pearls of an ordinary type."

The police officer nodded emphatically.

"Exactly," he said. "That is why the pearls are remarkable, and that is why at Scotland Yard we are anxious about them. They are pearls which would sell anywhere—in Paris, New York, Buenos Ayres; the very collection that would tempt Chicago Kate," he said slowly and with emphasis.

Redwood was surprised and showed it.

"Is she in London?" he asked.

"According to our information, she is," replied Harrod. "You know of her, of course?"

Redwood smiled. She was the nightmare of every dealer in Hatton Garden. Didn't she steal the Grein diamond? Had she not taken Lady Dale Mortimer's emeralds? From one end of the jewellery world to the Other Chicago Kate was a terror and a menace.

"She has been over here for some time," the detective went on.

"Why isn't she arrested?" asked the other

"Because very few people know her," explained Harrod. "She is to most of us only a name. She hasn't been working for quite a long time. Now apparently she has turned up in London." He rose. "I came to warn you, as I have warned other gentlemen in your business. Take my advice and have your pearls sent to the bank."

So that was all the visit signified. In his relief Redwood felt almost cheerful.

"I am greatly obliged to you, Mr. Harrod," he said, walking to the door with his visitor.

Harrod looked round, his hand on the door. "Er—young lady," he said.

"Yes?" Margaret Marsden raised her pretty face to the Inspector.

"I'm afraid I've said a little more than I Intended," he said, half in jest. "You mustn't talk about what you have heard."

The girl smiled.

"I wasn't listening," she said.

"That's wise of you. Good night, sir."

"Good night, Inspector."

Harrod paused irresolutely.

"By the way, sir, you don't happen to know where I can find your partner?" he asked.

What did he want with Fenner?

"No, he's probably gone home," said Redwood. He had not seen Fenner that day; he was racing at Windsor, he believed. Fenner was always at races lately—that was one of the reasons why people had been so suspicious of the firm's stability.

Redwood waited till the door closed on the detective; then he walked slowly back to the desk, his agile mind busy with a thought. Suppose these pearls disappeared while Chicago Kate was in London! People would think— The thought was worth pondering. He looked across to the girl. She was pulling a sheet from the typewriter.

"Finished?" he asked.

"Yes," she replied laconically.

"Have you finished the copy of the letters I gave you?" he asked.

She shook her head.

"No, they will take me till late," she said.

She avoided his eye, this trim, pretty woman with the delicate hands and the gold-brown hair. He regarded her admiringly.

"You don't mind working alone in the office? On your birthday, too?" he asked.

She smiled a little.

"Not at all; I prefer it—even on my birthday," she said drily. He understood the emphasis she put upon one word.

"You mean that you're glad to see the back of me?"

"Exactly," she said briskly, and slipped a new sheet of paper into the roller of her machine.

"But, Margaret—" he protested.

"Don't 'Margaret' me, please," she said coldly.

He laughed.

"You're a cold-blooded devil. Why do you work here for two pounds a week when—"

There was no need for him to finish his sentence. She had grown weary of the repetition. The offer he had made her was such as had been made to a hundred women. God knows that Redwood was not in a position to offer even ten pounds a week, and the furnishing of the flat might at this juncture have presented certain difficulties.

She made no reply to his suggestion, her quick fingers stabbed the keys with bewildering rapidity, and he had to talk through the clatter she made.

"I swear to you that I love no other woman in the world," he said earnestly.

Clickety clickety, click clack.

"You don't believe me?"

She stopped.

"I don't believe you," she agreed shortly, "and I'm not greatly interested anyway."

"I would do the right thing," he pleaded.

She smiled as she rose to carry her work to Fenner's desk.

"When a man says that," she said quietly, "he has started off by doing the wrong thing. The right thing, I suppose, is the flat and the £10 a week for housekeeping."

Then it was he saw the little package on his desk.

"What's this?" he demanded, and unwrapped it. "Why, you've sent back the present I gave you!"

She nodded.

"Your little present is too expensive even for a birthday present. I'm greatly obliged to you all the same. It goes with the flat and the ten pounds a week, I imagine?"

"My dear girl!" he laughed.

"My dear man," mocked she, "don't you realise that if I wanted that sort of life there are a dozen people in the world who would give me a much bigger flat, and—let us say, twenty pounds a week, and much more expensive birthday presents!"

"But they wouldn't be me."

The complacence in the tone tickled her.

"That would make the prospect ever so much more pleasant," she said a little cruelly.

He shrugged his shoulders and looked up at the clock ticking soberly over the door. There were ten minutes before he need go; possibly the dinner with Sigley would be unnecessary—if he could persuade her. In his selfish way he loved her; and she was the more desirable because of her resistance. He walked over to the safe and unlocked it. The sight of the Lai Singh rope might inspire him to a course. She owed something to him. He had taken her into this office three months ago and given her a bigger salary than she had asked. He knew nothing about her; she might have been Chicago Kate for all he knew. He mentioned this fact.

"Chicago Kate?" she asked, puzzled.

"You know—the woman thief that detective was talking about. I took a risk when I brought you into one of the greatest firms of pearl merchants in Hatton Garden. I took a risk, by Jove!" he grumbled.

"And so did I, by Jove!" mocked the girl.

He had opened the safe and brought out the filigree silver box and placed it on his desk.

"Do you know what it contains?" he asked impressively.

"No," she responded.

It seemed that she was in no mood for small talk.

"It contains the Lai Singh pearls. There's £20,000 worth here."

She was not as obviously impressed as he could have desired.

"It seems a lot of money," sh.e said, and that was all.

"What would you do with £20,000?" he asked, with a smile.

"Me? "She considered. "I'd buy a new hat, I think."

Her sarcasm left him unamused. An idea was growing.

"Margaret, there's something I'd like to tell you," he said.

If she knew the truth she might throw in her lot with his. Women are curious creatures.

"There's something I'd like to tell you when you call me Margaret," she said hotly, but he took no notice of her indignation.

"I could offer you a new life," he said half to himself. "A life of ease and luxury in another land. By God, I've a good mind to take you into my confidence!"

"Don't!" She raised her hand warningly. "I don't want to know."

"Tell me. There isn't anybody else? Fenner?"

The contempt in her smile disposed of that sportsman.

"I know Fenner," he said. "He's my partner, but he's a wrong 'un. There isn't anything straight about him except his circumstances. Don't put your faith in Fenner. He's broke. Horses, and betting, and—worse."

"The greatest firm of pearl merchants in Hatton Garden, I think you said?" she asked.

He spread out his hands in deprecation.

"These things happen. Affairs have gone badly with us." He looked at his watch. "I shall miss my dinner," he said. "Good night."

"You're not taking your bag," she reminded him.

"No, that can wait."

She nodded.

"You've packed up. Are you going away somewhere?" she asked.

"No. I just"—he hesitated. Then: "Well, it is nothing to do with you anyway; you aren't interested."

She nodded, this time vigorously.

"Yes, I am," she said. "I am always interested when a prosperous pearl merchant packs his bag and books his ticket to the Continent."

"How do you know?" he gasped.

She picked up a square black cover from the desk.

"Here is the ticket," she said, with gentle malice. "You put it down and forgot to take it up in the agitation of your love-making."

He swore under his breath, and at the door turned.

"Oh, by the way, your typing needn't keep you," he said carelessly. "I may want the office later, and remember this, Margaret—"

"Oh, dear!" she protested wearily. What she had to remember she did not learn, for as Redwood stood with his hand on the knob of the door, Fenner came in. A smart man with a certain ruddiness of face that told of a life devoted to field sport. The race glasses slung over his shoulder suggested an explanation for his absence all day. He scowled at his partner.

"Hello!" he growled.

"Hello!" repeated the other ungraciously.

"I-came to get something out of my desk," said Fenner.

"Oh!"

Redwood's tone expressed, as if in so many words, that the explanation for the other's presence was not accepted.

"Going?" asked Fenner.

"Yes. I'm dining with Sigley."

Fenner grinned.

"Hope you have a good time," he said ironically.

Still Redwood lingered.

"Are you coming my way?" he asked more politely than usual.

Fenner was sitting at his desk eyeing his correspondence dubiously; now he looked up.

"No, not just yet. I've a letter or two to dictate. Many happy returns, Miss Marsden," he nodded to the girl.

"Thank you," she smiled.

"I'll wait for you," Redwood decided. "Miss Marsden wants to get away."

"Don't trouble," Fenner waved him to the devil. "They are private letters."

"Well, I'll wait," said Redwood.

He suspected the other of many things—but mostly of a partiality for this pretty girl at the typewriter.

"What the devil do you mean?" demanded Fenner. "If you don't understand that I'd rather have your room than your company you're more thick-headed that I thought you were."

"I don't know how thick-headed you thought I was," said the other coolly.

"Look here, Redwood—" Fenner rose angrily from his chair.

"Gentlemen!" It was the shocked Margaret.

"Perfectly beastly temper you've got, Fenner," complained Redwood. "Your horses been acting the fool again?"

"Mind your own business," said his sullen partner.

"I see by the papers that 'Molten Gold' was beaten by a short head for the Windsor Handicap," Redwood went on. He took up the paper he had brought in. "'Heavily backed and beaten on the post,'" he quoted. "That was unfortunate for you, Fenner, if you were the backer."

"There's lots of interesting news in the paper," snarled the other. "They say the South African market has slumped to blazes. Gilfontein Deeps are down to 20s. You held quite a parcel of Gilfonteins, Redwood."

Redwood shuffled awkwardly. So Fenner knew!

"Yes, I did," he admitted.

"That was unfortunate, too," sneered Fenner.

"I didn't expect the market to go as it has," replied Redwood in an injured tone.

His partner laughed.

"Nobody ever docs," he said. "I didn't expect 'Molten Gold' to be beaten by a short head this afternoon. These things happen."

There was nothing to be gained by waiting.

"Good night, Miss Marsden," said Redwood. And then: "Good night, Fenner."

"Night," growled the man at the desk without looking up.

Redwood slammed the door. As he did so Fenner rose.

"Maggie! "he said quickly, and she swung round.

"Now, Mr, Fenner," she warned, "I've told you I can't allow you to call me by my Christian name."

"It's probably the last time I will. I am in the devil of a hole."

She saw the haggard face; he had put off his mask of indifference. Here was a man immensely hurt.

"It seems an unfortunate day for the firm of Redwood & Fenner," said the girl not unkindly.

"But I'm not in such trouble that I haven't thought of you. I've brought you this," he said eagerly, and took a case from his pocket. "It's a little birthday present." She came over from her corner of the room and took the thing, opened it, and raised her eyebrows.

"A little birthday present! "she repeated "Why, that is worth a hundred pounds! "

"I forget," he answered carelessly.

"I suppose you haven't paid for it?" she said.

He frowned, then the humour of it struck him, and he laughed.

"That has nothing whatever to do with you," he said.

"How curious men are!" She closed the case and handed it back. "Here is your present," she said.

"What!" He was aghast. "You're not going to take it?"

She shook her head.

"No, thank you," she said. "I—er— can't afford to take it."

He was hurt now in his self-esteem—more vulnerable a part than his self- respect.

"Well, I can't force it on you," he said dourly.

"Besides," she smiled, "it may be valuable to you—now."

He drew a long breath.

"Oh, it will be valuable to me all right. I shan't be able to settle on Monday?"

"Can't you compromise?" she asked.

"No," he said bitterly. "I couldn't hold my head up again if I pleaded for time. I've got to clear out."

"I see—make an honourable bolt. What happens to your head, then?"

This Margaret could be very hard.

"Don't trifle, Maggie," he said.

"Miss Marsden," she corrected.

"Oh, well, if you want to be so infernally proper! I met Inspector Howard outside."

"He- came to warn you about Kansas Jane, or some weird person," she said.

"Chicago Kate. Yes. Suppose those pearls of ours disappeared—vanished in the night—" He laughed. He would not have been so amused had he known that the same idea had already occurred to his partner. "We should know where they'd gone, shouldn't we?"

"I should," said the girl, over her shoulder. "I should know that the partners of Redwood & Fenner were on their wav to the Continent."

He was startled.

"What do you mean?" he asked.

"You've brought your bag, too," said she. He had; though at the sight of Redwood he had put it down by his desk without ostentation.

"Yes, I—er—" he began.

"Packed? And a ticket in your pocket to Berlin or somewhere? "

"How did you know?"

"I guessed," she smiled.

He took two swift steps toward her and bent over her shoulder. There was a vibrant note in his voice as he spoke. Here was a stronger, more reckless passion than Redwood's. He gripped her arm.

"You know there's no girl in the world who is to me what you are," he said rapidly. "Take the plunge! I offer you a life of happiness, of freedom, new sights, a new life in another land. I want you! "

She got up quickly.

"Let go my hand, please," she said, and pushed him away. "How dare you!"

He laughed.

"How dare I? How dare I do anything? I'm ruined—so is Redwood. He's waiting for the opportunity to clear away with these pearls, the last valuable consignment with which we shall ever be trusted. Don't you think I know? They're insured; nobody will lose except the underwriters."

She had walked quickly to Redwood's desk—a solid bulwark between herself and this masterful man.

"Poor underwriters!" she said.

In a moment he had forgotten her in the larger enterprise.

"If I could be sure they would fix on Chicago Kate—" he considered aloud.

He had a trick of biting his fingers when he was perturbed.

"Poor Chicago Kate!" she said, watching him. "Must she be in the same cart as the underwriters?"

He shook his head slowly.

"I can't take the risk," he said definitely then. "You can go as soon as you like," he added briefly. The girl smiled, the tone was so different now.

"You'll remember this birthday!"

"I shall."

Fenner crossed to the safe and opened it, he pulled out the filagree box and brought it to his desk.

Margaret, watching him curiously, asked : "What are you going to do?"

"I must take my chance," he said.

From his key ring he took a small key.

"Suppose I go to the police?" she asked quietly, and he laughed.

"Accuse me of robbing myself? Don't be silly!"

He found the key and slipped it into the tiny lock.

"Suppose I am accused?" she asked suddenly.

"You!" He was astounded at the suggestion, and inclined to be amused, but she was serious.

"Yes, I," she nodded. "I am the last in the office. They might arrest me as an accessory."

It was a sane objection such as you might expect Margaret with her clarity of vision to offer.

Fenner thought he could settle that for her. It did not matter a straw one way or the other to him. The world would know to-morrow. He sat at his desk and wrote:

"I, George Kenner, hereby certify that I removed the Lai Singh pearls, and that I have decamped with them."

He read the words aloud as he wrote them.

"That will satisfy you," he added, and handed the paper to the girl.

"But not me!"

Fenner swung round with an oath. Redwood stood in the doorway looking very white—the white of murderous passion. He had heard and he had understood the significance of the scene.

He hated Fenner at that moment as he never hated a man in his life. Hated him for his treachery and because of the girl who had received his confidence.

"You treacherous hound!" he breathed. "Are you the only man in the world looking for escape?"

Fenner was dazed. He passed his hand in front of his eyes as though to wipe away something that obscured his vision.

"We're both in it, Redwood," he said hoarsely. "I was mad. Can nothing be done to avoid this? Why," the thought came to him suddenly, "you came back for them yourself!"

"What if I did? "Redwood asked sullenly. "Anyway, we share and share alike."

Margaret Marsden watched the little scene completely absorbed by its melodrama. Now, as Fenner went hastily to the safe, she asked: "What of me?"

"You?" asked Redwood.

"I!" she said. "You must put me right with the world. You shan't leave me to hear the stigma of being concerned in this."

Redwood remembered the letter his partner had written and frowned.

"She's right," said Fenner. "Give me that letter."

Margaret handed it back, and Fenner ran his pen through some words and substituted others. "Here you are," he said. "'We, George Fenner and Horace Redwood certify that we have removed the Lai Singh pearls and have decamped with them.'"

"That alteration will do. Sign it, Redwood. If we bolt to-night what does it matter?"

Redwood looked at her. Then he signed, and the girl took the letter and gravely blotted it. She lifted down her little hat which hung above the machine, threw the ends of a stole about her neck, and took up her muff. The two men were busy; noiselessly she opened the drawer of Redwood's desk.

"There's a train leaves Waterloo to-night at ten," Fenner was saying. "Southampton at midnight, arrives at Havre at day-break."

"That's the train," said the other.

Fenner looked at his watch and opened the filigree box.

"We've time to share these up now. Why, Chicago Kate wouldn't have done this job neater!" he added, with a grin.

"Stop!" It was the girl who spoke; her left hand fell upon the box, aud with one swift movement she drew it toward her. She stood between the two men at the far end of the desk.

"You are insulting Chicago Kate. She would not do this job so clumsily."

"You seem to know a great deal about her," said Redwood, recovering from a momentary spasm of alarm.

"I do," she said quietly, "for I am Chicago Kate! Don't move, my amorous friends," she went on, dropping her voice, "with your twenty pound flats and your new lauds and your new joys. I'll shoot the first man that gives me trouble."

The revolver she pointed was undoubtedly Redwood's taken from his drawer.

"Why, you don't mean—" Redwood was floundering in amazement. Fenner was dumb.

"I am Chicago Kate," said the girl quickly. "I came here for a job, because I was tired of the work I had been doing. I wanted to start straight in a new land. I came to a jewel store because I love jewels. But you didn't give me a chance," she almost wailed. "It was love, flats, and allowances, and journeys to the Continent, birthday presents of £100 for a poor typist. You've shown me that there isn't a chance for a pretty woman in this game, so I'm going back to America. I shan't steal any more. I've enough to live on—now."

She lifted the box and tucked it under her arm, her fanning revolver covered the men.

"Ha!" Fenner heard the quick footsteps on the stairs, but not before the girl had heard.

"Don't move! Don't speak!" She shut and locked the door.

"Mr. Redwood! Mr. Redwood!" It was Harrod's voice.

"The police! By God, we've got you!" Redwood cried triumphantly.

The girl lifted a letter and waved it before him.

"'We, George Fenner and Horace Redwood hereby certify that we decamped with the Lai Singh pearls.'" She smiled her mockery.

"My God!" Fenner saw the hopelessness of the situation.

"Mr. Redwood, are you there?" Harrod outside was growing impatient.

"I'm going to open the door," she said in a low voice. "I can shoot through my muff very easily."

She turned the key noiselessly and Harrod came into the room in a hurry.

He looked from face to face and smelt a row; but he saw only the element of a vulgar misunderstanding in which a woman had played a part.

"I'm sorry to intrude," he said, "but I've just had a message from Scotland Yard to say that they believe the story of Chicago Kate being in the City is untrue."

"Untrue!" said Redwood, and caught the girl's eyes.

"So that relieves you of anxiety," said Harrod.

Fenner nodded.

"Good night, Mr. Redwood," said Margaret. With the box under her arm she made for the door leisurely.

"I—" Redwood began in a strangled voice. She showed him a folded sheet of paper.

"I have this letter," she said sweetly. "I'll make a copy of it in the morning."

She had to pass Harrod with the jewels under her arm. He took a step toward her and Fenner's heart leapt to his mouth.

"That's a pretty box you've got, miss," said Harrod.

She smiled.

"Yes, isn't it? "she drawled. "It is my birthday to-day, Inspector, and my employers have given me a little birthday present. Haven't you?"

The two men nodded speechlessly.

For a moment she stood in the doorway, and then the gallant Harrod felt moved to offer her a good exit.

"Many happy returns," he said, and bowed.

Three minutes later she was in a taxicab speeding West, and two men stared at one another across a common desk.

"She ought to, have been a member of the firm," said Fenner, and laughed hollowly.

The Despatch Rider

I

Lady Galligay was always always starting things: other people usually carried them on, complaining bitterly the while that they had ever been born to assume the responsibilities which Lady Galligay created. For the "things" that she started with such zest invariably ended and finished without any assistance whatsoever. They faded away without violence and without noise. In January all Tadminster would be talking of Lady Galligay's newest project; there would be drawing-room meetings innumerable. They might even develop shape as a "cause," and attain to thc dignity of a public meeting, recorded in large type in the Tadminster Times. But by April, so feeble would the flame of interest flicker, that it was a case of "By the way, what happened to that great scheme of Lady Gally's?" when men and women met.

The Tadminster Mounted Nurse and Despatch-Rider Corps was one of this feather-brained little lady's most brilliant inventions. She was forty, and vague. and rich, and immensely energetic, and if she lacked stamina it was not to be expected that all the virtues of organization should dwell in one small body. It was after her "Cottage and Pigsty" for the democracy had been rejected by the same democracy, although two cottages were built and a whole drove of pigs had been mobilized, that Lady Galligay had planned her Mounted Nurses' Corps. It was an idea—even George Mestrell agreed that it was an idea, but, of course, he never dreamt that Jo would take up with the beasly thing. If the truth be told, Jo was rather aghast at finding herself enrolled, but Lady Gally was so awfully plausible, and well, there it was; George must take the situation as he found it, or leave it.

George, full of good spirits, came down from Aldershot one Saturday in spring, bringing, so to speak, the good news from Aix, for there had been an unexpected resignation and he had got his company. It made all the difference in the world, because matrimony was not encouraged amongst subaltern officers. He was entirely full of his good news, and sat on the edge of the settee in the dinky little drawing-room of Nearminster House, and told Gresham, demure and beautiful, her tender grey eyes smiling approval of her soldier lover and his enthusiasm, waited to impart her own news.

She broke it obliquely, with a line pretense of unconcern. Instinctively she felt, or he felt, that there was something in Lady Gallagay's latest which was not quite—

"I suppose you've heard of Lady Gally's corps?" she asked, carelessly.

He had a trick of smiling with his eyes which ordinarily was very pleasing. For the first time in their acquaintance it failed to disarm her. Rather it sent her heart sinking down and down.

"Why do you smile?"

"I read something about it in the papers," he laughed. What a dear, funny old bird she is! Not a bad idea, hut imagine a corps of attractive young women gallivanting over a modern battlefield!

"In the sacred cause of humanity," she said. She knew she was being horribly trite, and felt no sweeter in consequence.

He stared up at her solemnly, for she had risen and stood, a slim, heroic figure, her rebellious chin tilted up, her fine brows set in menace.

"You are a soldier and you are biased," She went on, slowly. "You don't realize how women's positions have changed, how their capacities have enlarged. You don't underrtand.

Now the curious thing was, as she admitted to herself, that she herself had thought the corps a little ridiculous, and on the first "parade" she had felt so self-conscious as to vow a vow never again to appear in public so arrayed. But now, encountering a half-anticipated opposition, her attitude of mind had changed, and she indulged herself in a veritable orgy of inconsistency. She was unreasonably angry with him.

"Wait!" she commanded, suddenly, and whisked out of the room.

He waited, frowning his bewilderment, a neat, cleanly soldier man. How like Jo to jump down his throat for nothing at all! She was the dearest and sweetest and most perverse and obstinate of girls, and why on earth she should champion Gally the Lord only knew. So he thought, and, thinking, wondered why she had left him so dramatically.

After ten minutes' wait, ten minutes in the course of which he was by turn angry, amused, alarmed—suppose she was crying over something he had said—and resigned, he heard her footsteps on the parquet of the hall, and rose as she entered. He had had no intention of rising, because George's manners were deplorable, as everybody in Tadminster knows, but he rose—and gasped.

She came into the room, closing the door behind her, and stood, a little flushed, a little defiant, confronting him. Upon her pretty head was a wide sombrero hat, which was fastened under her chin by a strap. She wore a tight-fitting tunic blouse of blue cloth, with two rows of silver buttons; a skirt of serge braided in scarlet, which reached only so far as midway between knee and ankle; patent leather riding boots; and a suggestion of dark blue riding breeches went with snow-white haversack, military cross-belt, and riding gauntlets to complete the picture.

For a moment there was silence; then he spoke.

"Fancy dress or something?"

She pressed her lips tightly together and shook her head. There was a light in her eyes which should have warned him.

"What is the joke?" he asked, earnestly. "Is it private theatricals?"

She withered him with one glance.

"This is the uniform," she said.

"The uniform?"

"Lady Galligay's Mounted Nurses and Messengers," she explained, with unnatural patience.

He looked at her from head to toe, and in his scrutiny there was to Jo something unpardonably offensive.

"But," he said, slowly, "you're not rowing in that galley, dearie—dash it all, I mean you're not one of those infernally sill—I mean one of those?" He blundered himself to a standstill.

"Go on, please," she encouraged him, though her eyes were very moist and she was biting her very red lips with unnecessary vehemence.

"But, my girlie, it's so dashed absurd!" He blurted out the truth in his despair, this tall young man (something of a strategist in another field).

"Absurd?"

"I mean," he floundered, "it's so jolly theatrical, and the girls look such guys, and—"

"Thank you."

"But don't you see," he protested, "you can do nothing—you can't gallop about on a battlefield, darling; it isn't done. What can you do? You can't carry wounded soldiers about on horseback; and, as for despatch-riding, who the dickens is going to take order from you?"

"I can—we can do many things," she said, firmly and coldly; "but it would be foolish of me to argue the matter—I think you are just horrid, and I hate you!"

He stood in the centre of the room after she had flounced out, and for exactly three minutes he was penitent. Then he became annoyed, and when a tight-lipped and wholly antagonistic maid had informed him curtly that Miss Josephine was not to be seen, he was very angry indeed, and went back to town by the next train.

And that was the beginning of a tactless correspondence between two young people, a correspondence in which the effect of a certain scrappy tenderness was utterly annihilated by the indiscriminate use of notes of exclamation.

Jo resigned her membership of the Flying Nurses, gave her uniform to the gardener—an unimaginative man who saw possibilities for little boys' breeches in the voluminous riding-skirt—and she went abroad on the long-planned motor tour through South-Western France, previously dispatching a half-hoop of diamonds with a curt note to "Lieutenant G. Mestrell, 1st Southamptonshire Regiment, Talavera Barracks, Aldershot." And this though George had explained to her the highly important fact that he had secured his captaincy.

Of her adventures, her spasms of remorse, of letters reproachful and letters affectionate and letters completely penitent which she wrote and tore up, it is not necessary to tell. She lost her girl companion at a little town between Paris and Orleans.

Of her adventures, her spasms of remorse, of letters reproachiul and letters affectionate and letters completely penitent which she wrote and tore up, it is not necessary to tell. She lost her girl companion at a little town between Paris and Orleans.

There were rumours of war in the air, but that was no unusual experience in France. Bertha Mansell, however, was nervous, and must go home, and Jo was left with her little two-seater to decide whether she should take the Paris-Amiens road, or whether she should continue northward to the old-world town of Senlis. Here in the heart of the country an aunt had a little château. Jo decided on the second course, and came to the Château Verte to find herself its sole occupant, Aunt Martha having been bitten by the war scare and having left in a hurry for England.

It suited Jo, this month of absolute rest after the strenuous days of motoring. She sketched and slept and listened with amusement to the wild stories of war which an ancient French servitor and his no more youthful spouse regaled her with.

Then one day she awoke with a shock to learn the truth. There was war. Motoring out towards Beauvais, she had seen French soldiers marching northward. Belgium had been invaded, Liège was in their hands—even Brussels, they said, but that was unbelievable. Yes, it was possible to get to Ostend, but she must hurry.

The English were also at war, they told her, but only on the sea. She felt a sudden lightening of heart at this—hugged the obviously unlikely story to her heart, though reason told her that one Service could not be engaged without the other.

She hurried hack to the château, packed her traps, and strapped them to the rear of her little car. The servitor and his wife had already made preparations for departure.

"Take the road through Maubeuge, and branch off to Condé, mademoiselle," said the man; "but" — his face was troubled — "it would be better to go to Calais; that is only five hours away."

She shook her head.

It was a perfectly absurd consideration. but she had come to the Continent by way of Ostend, and had her return ticket by that route. Moreover, there was a rebate to be claimed at the frontier; a rebate of the provisional duty she had paid on her car.

Besides, she might see something of the fighting—an exhilarating and joyous thought. She set her car at the hill which led from the château to the plateau above Senlis with a sense of glorious anticipation.

II

Over by Condé the guns were sobbing fitfully. You had to listen with your ears strained to catch the insistent note. If you climbed to the high belfry of St. Peter's you saw, through good glasses, little woolly balls of smoke appearing in the air, saw the shapeless drift of it as it thinned, and, listening with all your nerves tense, you might identify one of the far-off sobs with that lazy smoke spume.

"I think mademoiselle had better go quickly." The old priest, his cassock white with the dust of the roads, was hollow-eyed and weary. His shoes were hard and burnt and grimy, and there was a two-days' stubble of beard on his chin. He stood by the side of the girl in the bellry, plucking at his lip thoughtfully, his anxious eyes divided between the northern horizon and the slim girl by his side. Jo was young and immensely pretty—not the rose and cream prettiness of England, but the old-ivory beauty of the South. The eyes were big and grey and wide set, her mouth small but full-parted now in her excitement. The rough tweed dress, the short skirt, and puttied ankles suggested a bicycle, but it was a little two-seater "Mombo" that stood by the porch of the old church, a worn trunk strapped to the carrier. Altogether, thought Father Pierre, an incongruous figure in this area of horrible war. Her trim hat appeared grey—it had once been a most uncompromising black, but the roads of Southern Belgium in July are inclined to revolutionize the intentions of the modiste. "They are returning this way," said the priest, after a while, and fidgeted nervously. "Mademoiselle must abandon her idea of crossing Belgium—her way lies through Lille to the coast. She will be safe, for the English hold—"

"The English?" she gasped. "Are there English here?"

He nodded and smiled.

"There is a great division—there." He pointed towards Condé. "Also there are others in the rear."

"But they told me— Are you sure, father?"

He nodded again.

He was very sure, for had he not seen the yellow coats go swaying past through Rheims—yellow coats open to show grey-blue shirts and bare brown throats.

"The regiments?" He shook his head regretfully in answer to her question.

"No, I do not know the regiments. They wore badges—here, on the collar. Some had tigers in brass, one had a sphinx in white metal, some wore little grenades, and one had a bronze fox—"

"A bronze fox!" she gasped.

There is only one regiment in the British Army that wears the "red fox," and that is the Southamptonshire Regiment—that famous fox which they won in the Nepalese War. It took her a second to decide. Somewhere over there where the guns were going "glang!" "glang!" was George— George unreconciled—in danger.

She must see him. She must tell him she was sorry. It was the maddest of ideas. She knew how absurd it was even as she went stumbling down the belfry steps, followed by the startled curé. "No, mademoiselle!" he cried, in apprehension, as she turned the car to the northern road; "not that way— not that way!"

But with a cheery wave of her hand she put the little car to the long, straight road which led towards those dreadful guns.

She passed soldiers busily entrenching, French cavalry stealing along the side of the road. Once she slowed down before a cottage where a bare-armed surgeon was busy with the wreck of a man that lay stretched on a big kitchen table, They glanced at her curiously, but did not stop her. Then there was a clearer stretch of road, and she let out the little Mombo to its top licks. The guns were nearer now, their "boom-boom" was incessant, there was a horrible sound in the air—a whining, whistling, shrieking sound, and once she saw a white house far away to her right burst into flames and crumble slowly to pieces.

She passed through a tiny village which was still blazing. Men and horses lay by the side of the road in curious, unreal attitudes. They had been dragged to the side to allow a battery of artillery to pass. Later she was to see the shattered limber of one of these guns in a ditch with the feet and legs of a French soldier protruding from the wreck. It was as though he had crawled underneath to investigate the cause of the trouble—only he was so terribly still, and the girl went white and felt deadly sick.

She recovered herself with an effort, stiffened her back till she sat bolt upright, and grasped the wheel more firmly.

Then she came suddenly upon more soldiers lying by the side of the road, and occupying the centre of the broad roadway, at a place where it topped the hill before dipping again to the valley, a group of mounted men. She knew it for the general staff of a French division. They were pointing to the left, and two of the officers were looking through their glasses. The girl stopped the car behind them. Here the roads branched off. A cross-road to the left led to Mons, as she knew; the one to the right would take her to Charleroi. But she realized she had reached the end of her journey. Here was Authority, which would send her back the way she had come. For the moment the staff were too occupied to notice her.

The dapper little general with the gold-laced képi was talking sharply, impatiently, to his chief of staff.

"Send a messenger at once to withdraw that company," he rapped. "Mon Dieu, it will be annihilated! The English have retired also. It is madness."

"I think they have—" began the other, when he was interrupted.

A group of soldiers were reclining by the side of the road. One had a small telephone receiver to his ear, and a trailing wire from a post above led down to him.

As the staff officer spoke one of the group rose and came towards the general with a slip of paper in his hand. He reached up the slip, saluting, and the general scanned the message.

"Cannot communicate with a company of the Southamptonshire Regiment on my right," he read. "Can you reach Captain Mestrell and order him to retire?"

For a moment the girl in the car swayed backward and forward; for that space of time the rush and roar of battle faded into a far-away buzz.

"Send a cyclist—it is risky." She heard the general speaking. "Tell the Englishman to take the road back to the hills by the stone cross. There's a way out for him."

She saw a young officer leap into the seat of his dirty motor-cycle, heard the pat-pat-pat of the engine, and watched him like one in a dream as he streaked down the hill to the right.

She watched him fascinated, gradually receding from view, then suddenly the cycle swayed left and right as though the driver were trying to evade some invisible obstacle. With one final lurch, cycle and rider went crashing to the ground,and the messenger did not rise.

"Send another man."

The curt tone of the general came to her.

Again an ofhcer mounted and went whizzing down the hill. He reached the bottom before, without warning, he went tumbling over and over till at last he lay an inert little bundle of humanity under his broken machine.

The girl heard the impatient click of lips.

"I can't risk another man. The road is swept by rifle fire."

They were going to leave him—to leave George and his men! Her eyes opened wide in horror at the thought. Yet she knew that the general was just.

"He will stay there till he is cut up," said the staff officer's voice, very slowly and deliberately. He had a solemn, mournful voice, she noted mechanically. She wondered in a numb, cold-blooded way if he were married. He spoke like a father of a family. A stout man, who sat his horse ungracefully. And George was to be left—to be cut up.

The car still purred and trembled under her. The wheel on which her hand rested shivered at intervals, as though it was part of a living, reasoning organism, dreading the ordeal ahead. She did what she did without thought. She gently pressed her foot downward, and the car moved.

"Stop! Who are you, madam?" It was the general, swinging round on his restive horse.

She could not speak; she could only point to the road that lcd to Mons.

She heard a warning shout, a cry of command, but they were too late to stop her.

Gathering momentum with every turn of its wheels, the little Mombo leapt down the hill. Her eyes were fixed on the road ahead. The first dead man she could pass without difficulty. She must slow to the next and go round him, and that was the danger point. She flew past the first obstacle, caught a fleeting glimpse of a doubled-up figure and a white face that stared up to the blue heaven, then the glass wind-shield smashed into a thousand pieces, and her lap was filled with splinters of glass. But she was not hit; only one flying splinter had drawn blood from her gloved hand. She was cool now, steadied the car for the man who lay in the middle of the road, and breathed a sigh of relief when she found that she had misjudged the space. There was room enough to pass. One sorrowful glance she gave to the pitiful thing which a few minutes before had been a living, breathing man, and then she began the ascent of a stiff little hill. And all the time she heard the smack, smack of bullets as they struck her car. She saw the off-side lamp jump up and fall, and once there was a sensation as though somebody had breathed a sharp, cold breath before her face.

On the crest of the hill she had immunity from danger. She ran through a cutting for half a mile, then the road turned suddenly, and she saw at the foot a rugged line of men retiring by short, sharp rushes from cover to cover. She heard the shrill whistle of an officer, and the line came with a run over the stubble field to the deep road. At full speed she sent the car forward, laughing and crying, for she had distinguished the tall young man in command, had indeed picked him out five hundred yards away.

Captain George Mestrell, unshaven and grimy, heard the wheels of the car and turned as the tiny two-seater jarred to a standstill.

"My God!" he breathed. "Jo!" She was still laughing, though her face was wet with tears.

"There is a road behind you," she cried, shrilly, "in the wood by the stone cross, and you've got to retire at once. The general says so."

"Jo!" he repeated, and pressed his hands before his eyes.

"The road by the stone cross," she said. "Look, look! there it is; I'll show you." She ran the car farther along the road till she came to the stone cross. There was little sign of road, only an opening in the thick bush which apparently led to the hill above, but she turned the car, and turned again, and struck a smooth track which wound between the densely-planted trees round the base of the hill on the left. She looked behind her. The men were following, and George, limping painfully, was with them.

"It is very wonderful," admitted a wholly mystified young officer a little later when a French surgeon had finished dressing an ugly bullet wound in his leg. "Can you tell me in what capacity you are serving?"

She smiled mysteriously.

"Lady Galligay's corps has been mobilized," she answered, untruthfully. And George winced.

Three War Stories For Children

Chapter I

Sentry No. 1

When Ferdie van Wyk was arrested for being found in the barracks of the Larkshire Regiment under suspicious circumstances, he very naturally objected to being marched through the one little street of Simon's Town by a military escort.

Ferdie was neither black nor white, being of that complexion which is described politely as "colored." He had been thrown out of Cronje's army for drunkenness and theft, and he had tasted the dread "sjambok"—that pliant length of rhinoceros hide which the backveldt Boer wields with such skill. He left, vowing vengeance upon his onetime friends, and came to the British Army at Modder River with a cock-and-bull story which secured him a post, first as transport rider, then as guide to the force. Here he was detected in the act of cruelly and unnecessarily flogging a native boy. The boy was a Fingo lad engaged as "voertrekker"—that is to say he walked ahead of an ox-team. leading them, since, as you may know, oxen are not guided by reins, and move so slowly that the "voertrekker" finds no difficulty in keeping ahead of them. For his cruelty, Van Wyk was kicked out of the British Army and carried himself to Commandant Viljoen, who was operating in the Free State. In his malice he volunteered to lead the Boers to an unprotected British post on the railway line between the Orange and the Modder Rivers.

He was so plausible with his stories of rich stores guarded only by a handful of soldiers that the commandant took his command to the attack, only to be repulsed with considerable loss. Van Wyk escaped with his life and wandered about the country, robbing isolated farmhouses and terrifying the women who had been left behind till he found himself at De Aar, in the Cape Colony, where he was suspected of having wrecked a troop train, but escaped again by smuggling himself on a southward-bound mail train.

He drifted to Simon's Town, filled with hatred for mankind and especially soldier-kind. It mattered little to him whether the soldier were Briton or Boer, whether he wore khaki or the cartridge belt which constituted the sole uniform of the burgher army.

A tall broad-shouldered man with a dark yellow complexion, flat nose and seamed cheeks, his sullen eyes surveyed the pretty little town hatefully. Like many other men who by their own wicked acts have brought punishment upon their heads, he blamed everybody but himself, and he blamed nobody so much as the deputy chief magistrate of Simon's Town, who, eight years before, had sentenced him to a term of imprisonment for atrocious cruelty to a dog.

It was unfortunate for Van Wyk (that was the name he adopted) that his thieving propensities should get the better of him. Thinking that the detachment of soldiers stationed in Simon's Town was engaged in manoeuvring on the hills, he made a furtive visit to the barrack-rooms, and was captured whilst he was pilfering a soldier's kit-bag.

Van Wyk scowled as he was led into the courthouse, for sitting on the bench was the same young magistrate who had sentenced him eight years before.

Mr. Gerald was not so young, but he bad scarcely altered, indeed he looked younger.

"I know your face," he said, when the evidence had been given; "aren't you Ferdie Van Wyk?"

"No," lied the prisoner, sullenly.

"I am satisfied that you are," insisted the magistrate.

"That's right, your worship," said a gaoler.

Van Wyk scowled at the official, and if a look could have killed, assuredly the gaoler would have died on the spot.

"I shall send you to Cape Town for trial," said the magistrate, and there the matter ended.

Outside the courthouse Van Wyk waited under the care of two armed guards, planning methods of escape. He saw a native nurse wheeling a baby up and down in the shade of the magistrate's garden.

"Whose child is that?" he asked in Dutch.

"The magistrate's little girl," was the reply. A malevolent gleam lit the halfbreed's eye as they marched him away to the cells.

He found himself locked up with two choice spirits, men of his own color, also awaiting trial, and both of them apparently foredoomed to long sentences.

"I wish I could take a match and blow this town off the face of the earth," said one bitterly.

"If we could set fire to the magazine," said the other.

Van Wyk, his heart filled with black hate, said nothing, but he thought of the magistrate and he thought of the gaoler.

"I have a plan, brothers," he said after a while. "At what hour does the gaoler come in the evening?"

"At seven."

"Alone?"

"Sometimes," said one of the men, "but he never enters the cell—he puts the food through, this trap," and he indicated a small wicket in the aoor.

"Where does he carry his keys?" asked Van Wyk

"On his belt."

Van Wyk thought. He was a man of tremendous strength, and his long arms, reaching almost to his knees, were more like a monkey's than a man's. He measured his arm against the door and nodded, satisfied.

At night came Crumps, the gaoler, with the evening meal. He came alone, but he felt safe enough with a door of thick oak between himself and his prisoners. He passed the bread and soup which formed the evening meal through the wicket, then as he was on the point of closing the little steel grating Van Wyk called him.

"What do you want?" asked the gaoler testily.

Van Wyk's arm shot through the wicket, and his long sinewy fingers caught the gaoler's throat. The man struggled, but was drawn to the grating, and another hand grasped him and drew him tighter to the door. He struggled madly, tore at the encircling fingers, but the assault was too sudden. He went limp and unconscious.

Van Wyk held him thus, then, gripping him by the collar with one hand, thrust his long arm through the wicket and found the keys hanging by a chain. With a wrench he tore the chain from the belt and let the inanimate figure fall to the ground.

He chose a key and reached bis arm through to its fullest extent... A minute or two later three prisoners tiptoed down the stone corridor to freedom and vengeance.

It wanted a quarter to one when the sentrv on No. 1 post began his weary perambulation of the beat which extended almost from the seashore to the iittle waterfall in the kloof. Behind the square, squat magazine the hill rose steeply. Above, the sentry heard the whine and the bark of baboons at their play. It was not a cheery post, even in the broad light of the African day, when Simon's Bay, alive with grey-hulled men-of-war brought a sense of companionship: at night No. 1 was the saddest of all posts in the world. So thought Terrence Cane as he shifted his rifle from one shoulder to the other for comfort, and stepped briskly toward the town end of his beat.

There was a level width of road cut out of the hillside. On his left now the ground sloped away steeply, leading down to a brook and a score of disreputable houses which were huddled about the insalubrious streamlet.

He was half-way across the road when he stopped suddenly.

Somewhere close at hand he had heard the whimper of a baby. It came from the left, and he peered down the slope. He saw a movement, ever so slight, on the hillside and brought his loaded rifle down to his hip with a smack. "Halt! who comes here?" he challenged quickly, but there was no reply. He listened. Only the barking on the hill and the musical tinkle of the fall broke the silence of the night.

Then again came the fretful cry and again he saw a movement.

He stepped carefully down the rough slope, his bayonet glittering blue in the moonlight, then with an exclamation stooped and picked up a little bundle that lay at his feet.

It was a little baby apparently only a few months old.

He climbed back to his post, carrying rifle in one hand and the baby in the other.

"Why, you little beggar!" exclaimed Private Cane reproachfully. "What do you mean by being out so late at night?"

It was a white child, beautifully and delicately dressed in night-clothes of the finest texture. How had it come there?

Ten minutes before he had thought he heard voices coming from the direction of the brook, but that was not an unusual circumstance. One always heard voices on No. 1 post, and before now the guard had marched to the relief of a sentry who had broken down into a nervous wreck from the strain of two hours spent on the magazine guard.

Cane walked slowly back to the magazine sentry-box. It was a warm night, but his overcoat hung there in case of rain, and he carefully wrapped the little one in its folds. She was sleeping as calmly as though she were in her beribboned cradle.

He was bending over the child when he heard a noise behind him. He turned quickly, but not quickly enough.

A billet of wood came down on his defenseless head, and he went down like a log.

"Better kill him and finish it," said Van Wyk

"What's the good," whispered the ruffian with him; "if we blow up the magazine he'll die without trouble—you were mad to leave the child on the hill."

Van Wyk turned with an oath.

"What else could we do?" he asked fiercely. "I didn't know he went so far in his walk—I didn't want to alarm him, and I can't carry a kid in mv arms whilst I'm scaling a magazine wall."

He looked at the senseless soldier at his feet, and the third man spoke.

"Let us take his rifle," he said.

"Time for that later," said Van Wyk gruffly. "Give me the matches and the shavings and help me over the wall."

But first they dragged poor Cane to a sitting position, bound him tightly with a length of cord, and forced a stick gag into his mouth. Whilst they were doing this the baby raised a fretful cry.

"Hurry up!" said Van Wyk; "if the magistrate discovers the kid has gone he'll raise the town—and besides, the sentries are relieved in half ah hour."

The three men made for the wall as the dockyard clock struck one.

"No. 2.—All-l-l's well!"

Van Wyk heard the distant cry from the barrack sentry.

"No. 3. —All-l-l's well!"

Fainter came the answer from the store guard.

He knew that the men in the guard room would be waiting for No. 1 to respond, and if he did not answer a file of the guard would come at the double to discover why.

"Hurry!" he growled.

A small baby girl who wakes from a pleasant nap in the middle of the night and finds herself in the unaccustomed surroundings of a sentry-box swathed in a soldier's great-coat may choose between yelling her indignation or investigating.

Baby Gerald investigated. She crawled from her bed and flopped alarmingly in the road. She saw a huddled man apparently asleep, and since she had seen people asleep before she was not alarmed. More to the point, she saw a very pretty object glittering on the roadway. It was a long rifle with a bayonet at its end, and she started to crawl its length, cooing cheerfully the while.

She started at the butt end and had not gone far when she stopped to investigate some highly-complicated mechanism. She did not know how complicated it was—all she realized was that it was inviting. She grasped at the polished bolt and she touched the magazine, and then her inquiring, saucy eyes saw a little projection of steel beneath tne rifle. She tugged at this, but it wouldn't come away. She turned again.

"Bang!"

Baby Gerald went backward with a terrified yell, and Van Wyk, astride of the wall, dropped quickly to the ground and ran for his life—straight into the arms of the hurrying picket.

He swung aside and darted down the slope, but the corporal of the guard was a crack shot, and Ferdie Van Wyk finished his earthly career on the slopes of Simon's Bay.

Baby Gerald is now a grown young lady, but they call her "Sentry No. 1" to this day.

Chapter II

The Pet of the Wigshires

There are regiments in the Army which are proud, and justly so, of certain regimental pets. One corps possesses a ram, another a deer, one a wolf-hound, and one at least claimed a bear that waddled ahead of the regiment. It is somebody's joy to lead the regimental pet with a white leather lead ahead of the band, and it happens in most regiments that that somebody is a drummer.

Now the Wigshire Regiment—its real name I will not give for obvious reasons—had no pet. They wore on their collars the Sphinx of' Egypt: but since no man had ever tamed a Sphinx to walk before a band, and since it must be a Sphinx or nothing with the Wigs—as they were called—the regiment treated the question of animated coats-of-arms with lofty contempt as something too childish to engage its attention.

It was lamentable that the Wigshires found themselves on four consecutive occasions with regiments favoured with divers representatives of the menagerie—lamentable for the reason that there began to grow up in the battalion a most pronounced feeling of dissatisfaction—and in no company was the discontent more strongly expressed than in the 'drums.'

Boy Steevens, a diminutive lad with a freckled face and a snub nose, was unusually bitter.

"There ain't no regiments in the Army, " he said, did this outrageous Boy Steevens, "that ain't got a dog or a goat or a performin' animal walking in front of the band—except us." There was a chorus of gloomy approval.

"You can't have a sp'inx, " protested Boy Carter, his mind running to logic, " 'cos there ain't no sp'inx—at least not a live one, an' the other regiments only have the animals that are on their collar badges."

This was apparently true, but did not help the drums to discover a solution to the difficulty.

"What's the nearest thing to a sp'inx?" demanded Boy Steevens suddenly.

This was a question which none present felt qualified to answer. A sphinx was unlike any representative of the animal world as could be imagined. A terrible problem indeed, and the Wigshires appeared to be doomed to oblivion if they depended for fame on a regimental pet which bore the slightest resemblance to the famed symbol of Egyptian oracle.

Suddenly there was a yell.

Boy Steevens, his eyes blazing with the splendour of his inspiration, had sprung up from the bed-cot upon which he sat. "I know," he cried, "I've got it."

The drums glared at him inquiringly.

"What?" demanded a dozen voices.

"A rabbit!" said Boy Steevens, trembling with excitement, "haven't you ever seen a rabbit—the same shape, the same funny look about its face, and his ears hangin' round his neck like the sp'inx. An' his two paws stuck out just like a sp'inx, an' waggin' his nose up an' down just like, I'll bet, a sp'inx did when he was alive!"

The drums were impressed. Even the most sceptical and cynical had to confess that there was some likeness.

"I'll bet, " said Boy Steevens rapidly, "that a sp'inx is only a skinned rabbit—we'll have a pet, an' I'll lead him."

But the voice of Boy Carter poured cold water on the proposition. "Rabbit ain't anything, " he said, "an' you can't train rabbits to walk in front of a band, because they don't walk—they just lop-lop this way an' that except when they're frightened. I know, " he added, "because I've kept rabbits."

But the drums had seized the idea and had adopted it as their very own with enthusiasm. A small baby rabbit was purchased secretly.

The drums undertook to train the rabbit in the way it should go. And when it was trained so that it should not stray from the straight path: when it had been taught—as Boy Steevens stoutly insisted it could be taught—to stand up on its hind legs and salute when 'God Save the King' was played, then that trained rabbit should be solemnly presented to the Colonel in full view of the regiment.

The training of the rabbit was a tremendous business. They trained him with bugles and they trained him with cabbage leaves, on the whole the cabbage leaves were the more successful. They marched in line (in the seclusion of a field two miles from barracks) blowing their bugles and the rabbit marched in front. He marched in front because they marched behind him. He did not go exactly in the way they wanted him to go, but they went the way he went, and when he stopped to munch grass they stopped too and pretended they intended stopping. They trained him lifting him by the ears, and they trained him by prodding him with a stick, and on the whole he went better when they carried him than when they prodded him.

But there came a day when Horace (for so they called him) really gave the impression that he had of a sudden realised his awful responsibilities; when he walked with stately lope before the frantic bugle march and—wonder of wonders—when it seemed that he understood that 'right turn' and 'left wheel' had some special significance for a marching rabbit.

It was time indeed for the secret to be revealed and for the presentation to be made.

There was a Commanding Officer's Parade due for the Wednesday, for the General commanding the district was coming to make his half-yearly inspection.

"Wednesday's the day," said Boy Steevens, a perspiring little figure as he sat on his cot polishing the brasses of his snowy belt. "Wednesday, chaps—or never."

He was inclined to be melodramatic, this Boy Steevens, and was given to the collection of cigarette pictures—sufficient evidence of a romantic soul.

Wednesday morning came, bright and spring-like, and no more gallant sight has ever been seen that the old barrack square presented with its great elms vivid with tender green, and the scarlet and white of uniforms upon the golden gravel of the square.

The regiment was drawn up in column, eight strong companies at intervals, and before them the drums in their white ribbon-lace and their epaulettes.

A shrill bugle call, and with a crash the rifles of the battalion came to the slope as the General in his cocked hat rode on to the square, followed by his staff. A sharp order and the rifles came to the 'present,' the bugles and the drums sounded the 'general salute.' One drum did not sound.

With a quick motion Boy Steevens raised the head of his drum and lifted out a struggling rabbit.

"Horace, do your duty.'" he hissed, and the sphinx of the Wigshires loped slowly forward till he crouched by the side of the drum-major. That officer was quite unprepared for the apparition . With a nervous little squeak he jumped sideways.

The obedient Horace, not unused to such gyrations, followed with two quick lopes.

The drum-major looked around helplessly. Very gingerly he prodded Horace with the end of his gorgeous staff.

"Get away, bunny", he cajoled, but at that moment came the Colonel's voice—"Battalion will advance in column. By the left—Qui-ck march!"

Crash, crash, crash went the drums of the Wigshires; the drum-major's staff spun round and the whole battalion stepped forward, their heads erect: their shoulders square. Horace leapt away at the first rattle of the drums, dashed madly a dozen paces, looked over his shoulder to see what had happened, and dashed as madly back again and fell in by the side of the purple-faced drum-major, loping steadily forward to the music.

"What the dickens is that strange beast, Colonel," asked the General as the troops swung past.

Colonel Umfreyville fixed his eyeglass. "Looks to me like a rabbit, sir," he said.

A smile broke the stern lines of the General's face—he was a notorious joker. "Do you know," he said drily,"I thought for one moment it was your sphinx.'"

Which shows that there is much in common between drummer-boys and Generals.

"Yes sir," said the tearful Boy Steevens when the parade was dismissed and he faced the laughing officers, "he's mine. I—I thought I'd train him for a regimental pet."

"You had better train him for your dinner-table," suggested the Colonel.

"No, no.'" said the General, who stood by, "that would be too bad; after all, I agree—he is not unlike the sphinx."

"Except that the Egyptian sphinx hasn't a ridiculous woolly tail, sir, said the Colonel, his lips twitching.

"Beg pardon, sir," interrupted Boy Steevens eagerly, "perhaps there's an English sphinx."

"I never thought of that," said the General gravely.

And thus the Wigshires adopted a regimental pet.

Chapter III

Frank the Trumpeter

From out of the mists ahead came three horsemen galloping quickly. They rose over the crest of a distant hill and disappeared into a hollow. A long interval, and then they appeared again, riding in line, erect as though on parade, seemingly oblivious of the fact that somewhere behind them an unseen enemy was 'sniping' them at his leisure.

Some of the bullets fell short and sent little fountains of earth spurting up from the ground. Some went overhead with a shrill whistle. One at least struck Birchington. Fortunately it was a ricochet that had lost much of its force. Yet it struck the steel stirrup with sufficient vehemence to twist his foot round.

He laughed quietly and did not draw rein. Birchington, a trumpeter of Birchington's Horse, was the youngest soldier in the field that day—was, indeed, the youngest soldier in the army serving in South Africa. Had he been a regular soldier he would have been left behind with the other boys at the base camp, for nowadays drummer boys do not go into the firing line, nor trumpeters of cavalry either, for the matter of that.

But young Birchington, though only fifteen years of age, was a favoured individual. His father, Colonel Birchington, had raised a corps which bore his name, a corps composed of young Colonials, with a sprinkling of English gentlemen who had come to South Africa on the outbreak of war on the off-chance of finding employment with the Army in the field. Colonel Birchington knew the country well. After he had resigned his commission in the British Army he had settled down to ostrich farming in South Africa with his young wife. She had died soon after Frank was born, and since that day the two had been inseparable—the hard fighting Colonel and his baby boy.

The authorities had accepted Colonel Birchington's offer to raise his corps, but had demurred when he suggested that his boy should accompany him in the field.

"He is very young, Colonel," said the Governor.

"That I admit, your Excellency, " said the Colonel firmly, "but the enemy have many boys of even a more tender age in the fighting line—a British boy can take the risk if they can."

The Governor smiled a little sadly.

"You must have your boy, " he said; "after all, you know how to take care of him."

So Frank Birchington, to his joy, became colonel's trumpeter to Birchington's Horse. There was no need for him to learn the calls. From his childhood he had possessed a little trumpet, and his father's servant taught him every call from Reveille to Lights out.

It was a proud boy who rode away from his father's farm to join the column. With his well-fitting khaki uniform, his long glittering sword at his side, a revolver strapped at his waist, and a polished brass trumpet at his back, he made a picture of which any father would be proud. From the toes of his brown top-boots to the crown of his broad-brimmed sombrero hat he was a soldier's son.

Now as he came galloping back to headquarters, a scout to the left and right of him, and the monotonous klick-klock of the Mauser rifles behind him, it seemed years since he had left the farm: it seemed another life that he had led before the call to war had come.

"Get over to the left, Frank," said one of his companions a little anxiously as a bullet fell between them; "we shall have the kopje as a background and our khaki will not offer such a good target."

Obediently the boy turned his horse. He had learnt that bravery is one quality, and foolhardiness another, though they are often confused. There was nothing to be gained by taking unnecessary risks. His father had impressed this fact upon him in their first engagement.

Frank had stood up in a perfect hail of bullets.

"Lie down, Frank," his father called sharply. He himself was crouching behind a convenient ant-hill.

"I am not afraid, father," said Frank, exalted by the sense of danger.

"Am I?" asked his father quietly, and with a blush of shame the boy realised the arrogance of his courage, and sank flat to the ground.

"You've got to remember, my son," said the Colonel that night, when they sat together at their evening meal, "that you are only useful to your country so long as you are alive. In my old days we had a saying that 'dead heroes cannot peel potatoes.'

They took their meals together, for the Colonel was no spartan father who demanded that the difference in ranks should separate them.

Frank and his two comrades gained the lower slopes of the kopje and began to skirt it, and in half an hour they had reached the camp.

The Colonel rode out to meet them. "Well, my boy," he said with a smile, "you have had your first lesson in scouting, what do you think of It?"

"It was fine."' cried the boy; "that is the work I should like to do. It's awfully uninteresting here, dad— we've had two little skirmishes in ten days and neither lasted an hour.'"

The Colonel eyed him thoughtfully.

"I think we shall have all the fighting we want very soon," he said, but would say no more.

Birchington's Horse, with a battalion of infantry and three guns, moved out the next evening for a destination which was known only to the Colonel. He did not share his confidence with Frank, because boys are boys after all, and an indiscretion on Frank's part might have jeopardized the column's safety.

The country abounded in spies; every farmhouse was a secret meeting place from whence news regarding the movements of troops was distributed to interested quarters.

It was against one of these farmhouses that Birchington's column was moving. In spite of Frank's disgust at the inactivity of the column Colonel Birchington had made himself extremely unpopular amongst the marauding commandoes. He moved swiftly and by the nearest way. He never lost his column amid the innumerable spruits and river-beds which abound in the country.

News had been received that a laager had been formed near Van Robeck's farm. A laager meant an armed camp, and it was believed that it formed part of the force of none other than the redoubtable De Wet.

Frank rode by his father's side in the darkness—they had not left the camp until the sun had sunk behind the big mountains to the westward.

They rode in silence for a while, the Colonel busy with his thoughts, and Frank too excited at the prospect of the coming fight to talk coherently He was an important factor in a night engagement. Infantry and guns moving out of sight in the gathering darkness would advance or wheel or retire at the sound of the brazen notes he blew—other forms of command were impracticable.

"Frank," said the Colonel suddenly, "you understand that to-night of all nights you take orders from nobody but myself."

"Yes, father," said the wondering boy.

"A night attack is a hazardous undertaking," the elder man said, "and it can only be carried out by one man. My orders to you are not to be countermanded. If I am wounded—yes, yes," he stretched out his hand and clasped the boy's knee affectionately, "these things happen—you are to take my last order and carry it out."

"I will, father," said Frank, blinking back the tears that rose to his eyes.

No more was said, for at that moment Major Galley-Bolder, second in command, rode up. The Major was one of those short, fussy men, irritable and apprehensive.

So far he had not shone in action; indeed, there were people who suggested that he had behaved with a caution bordering upon cowardice. He did not like Frank, and the dislike was reciprocated. He reined his horse alongside the Colonel's with an awkward tug of his reins, for he was not a good horseman.

"What is the idea of this march, Colonel?" he asked, endeavouring to disguise the irritation in his voice.

In a few words the Colonel enlightened him, dropping his voice so that the men who rode immediately behind could not overhear.

"I think a night attack is perfectly unjustifiable," said the Major hotly "It is endangering life which would not be endangered if the engagement were fought in daylight; hang it..."

"I do not think we need discuss that aspect of the matter," said the Colonel quietly; "the farm lies on the other side of Volkston Gap and the road leads through the Gap itself. If we can get through without opposition I shall put the guns on the hill to cover the farm and attempt to surround it."

"It's suicidal,"stormed the other; "why there may be a thousand burghers there..."

"And there may be a hundred," said the Colonel; "anyway, that is my plan."

The Gap was the key of the situation. As silent as ghosts the column approached it just as the dawn came east.

The gunnery officer had received his orders; with half a battalion of infantry he moved across the veldt to the right to take up a position on the hills, and the column halted to give him a chance of establishing himself. A mounted orderly brought news he had successfully reached the foot of the hill before the Colonel passed the word to advance.

It is said that in that period of waiting somebody (contrary to the strictest orders) struck a match to light a cigarette, and that that somebody was Major Galley-Bolder. Whatever happened, the enemy was warned.

As the head of the column deployed into the little valley a heavy fire broke forth from the left.

The Colonel breathed a sigh of relief. There was no sign from the right, the enemy had not divided his forces, and there would be opposition to the guns.

Frank's trumpet sent out a shrill order on the morning air and the column dismounted. Another call—and they were taking cover and replying steadily to the fire above.

The enemy's fusilade increased in vigour; they held a good position, and were, as the Colonel had feared, stronger than had been reported. Worse, they were moving stealthily along to flank his party. He moved ahead—there was no safer way, keeping a steady fire on the hill.

The guns should be in a favourable position by now and waiting orders.

Then as if by magic the firing on the hill ceased, and with a wild yell men broke from cover and came charging down the hill-side.

"Fix bayonets!" cried Colonel Birchington, and Frank at his side repeated the order. The onrush ceased. The men above had never intended charging—they desired only to take a more effective position, and this they had done.

The Colonel, with a sudden sinking of heart, saw his danger.

"Guns to open fire," he said sharply.

Frank's trumpet was half-way to his lips when he saw his father sway and fall. He was by his side in an instant.

"Father! Father!" he cried, but Colonel Birchington was dead, a bullet had pierced his heart.

Frank staggered back, white of face. Then he remembered his father's instructions and raised his trumpet.

A. hand grasped the instrument rudely.

"What are you doing?"

He turned to meet the livid face of the Major.

"Sound artillery retire, d'ye hear!" almost screamed the officer. "We're trapped. There is no way out of this!"

He wrung his hands in frantic despar.

"Sound it—we may get out—if they start shelling from the hill, they'll hit us.'"

Frank wrenched his arm free.

"I've had my orders, sir," he said, and his voice was broken and hard. He raised his trumpet and the clear thrill of the notes echoed from hill to hill.

"Stop!" cried the second in comnand. "I am in charge now, you young fool— what did you sound?"

"Commence firing," said Frank, and as he spoke three quivering pencils of flame leapt from the hill-side, and the crash of the artillery came like a thunder-clap.

The enemy wavered, the fire slackened instantly, and ere the guns spoke again the foe was in full retreat.

Yet the major had been prophetic, for although the fight was won, the first shell had fallen short, and father and son lay together in death, and near by was the stricken figure of the second in command.

Clarence — Private By Edgar Wallace

Chapter I

The Birth of the Sharpshooters

Fate played a low trick on a very bright boy when it named the younger son of Colonel Cassidy of the 184th (Winchester Regiment) "Clarence."

The horrid thing was that he looked "Clarence." He was a dear little boy whom, in his earlier youth, people persistently called a dear little girl. He had big solemn blue eyes and hair of ruddy gold. It was nevertheless the fact that, for all his angelic attributes, he had, when annoyed, a trick of saying things which made his victims? hair stand on end, though he was seldom rude and never vulgar. For this reason they christened him in the home circle "Clarence-with-the-awful-tongue."

At school they called him Mary Ann for just as long as it took to lick the school from Branger Major to "Moses" Flackery, for Clarence, despite his outward beauty, was bloody-minded, and had a left hook to the jaw that brought tears to your eyes. But amongst his own ken Mary Ann he remained, and Mary Ann he was to the end of his days.

At twenty he should have been in the Army—his father's last act in this life was to put the boy's name down for a regiment of the Guards—but somehow Sandhurst and he did not agree. He could box, run, swim, row and shoot. He played footer excellently and made forty-seven for Harrow one never-to-be-forgotten day at Lords. If proficiency in sport could qualify a man for a commission, Clarence would have had it, but for reasons best known to (a) the authorities, (b) his tutor, (c) Clarence, he was badly ploughed.

"Dear old fellow," he protested to George, the elder brother, and a major of Rifles, "why the deuce do I want to lumber my head with trigi-thigumy and that sort of rot? I couldn't do it at Harrow, dear old chap, and I can't do it at Sandhurst."

"Mary Ann," said the Major severely, "you're an ass." But for all his severity he said this in some fear, for he shared with the family a wholesome respect for the vocabulary of his youngest brother.

"I dare say, I dare say," admitted Clarence with his most angelic smile, "the fool of the family, dear sir and brother, somebody's got to be it. If they want a real dashin' officer I'm their man, but if they want a beastly brainy professor feller, I'm off the mat. That rotten old examiner had me counted out before half the round was through—knocked me out, sir, and hadn't the decency to give me a count."

George, broad-shouldered and red of face, grinned.

"What are you going to do, son?" he asked.

Clarence pushed his top hat to the back of his head and twirled his gold-headed cane. He was a picture of a youth, speckless and immaculate, and innocent, though of late years his jaw had broadened a little and there was, for the patient observer, more evidence of strength than effeminacy in his face.

"I don't know what I shall do," he said, and looked round vaguely as though expecting to find some inspiration in the solid furniture of the Junior Officers' Club. "Of course I've an idea that I'm cut out for a soldier. I bet I'd knock spots off that beastly old examining feller if it came to a rough and tumble on the gory field of battle. And as for strategy, believe me, I'm Moltke!" He shook his head wisely. "Wouldn't catch me doing frontal attacks. What the devil are you laughing at?"

"I wasn't laughing," replied Major George Cassidy, "I was crying."

He got up from his seat.

"You'll have to pass through, somehow, Mary Ann," he said seriously, as he grasped the boy's hand. "No footling!"

"Not a blooming footle!" said the other heartily.

George Cassidy hesitated.

"What are you doing to-night?"

"Dining."

"With?"

"A lady," said Clarence mysteriously, "a lady in high society."

George stared.

"How the dickens do you come to know her?" he asked coarsely.

"You'll discover one of these days," was the prophetic reply.

"Take my tip," said George at parting, "enlist. Go through the ranks. You'll get a commission all right—only—"

"Only what?"

"Don't join the 12th Rifles. You see, it would be jolly awkward—"

"Very," Clarence stopped his brother with a lofty wave of his hand. "Though you might be sure I shouldn't boast about it. Even a private soldier doesn't want to own up to some of his relations."

Manfred Cassidy, a lieutenant of the Irish Light Infantry, a rough edition of Clarence, came over to see him. He burst into the Jermyn Street flat one morning and found his brother in a flowered silk dressing-gown nibbling dry toast.

"Mary Ann," said he without any of the affectionate preliminaries which preface brotherly utterances in fiction, "George says they've chucked you out at Sandhurst."

"Neatly put," murmured Clarence. "Have some breakfast?"

"Horrible luck, old man." Manfred slapped him on the shoulder. "But I've got a jolly good idea."

"I'll have it framed," said Clarence, hugging himself tighter in his dressing-gown and gazing benevolently at the other.

"This is the idea," said Manfred, speaking rapidly and with great heartiness, "enlist as a private."

"Ah!" said Clarence politely.

"Only," Manfred hesitated, "perhaps it would be best not to join the Irish Light Infantry. You see, old chap, I'm getting my company next month, and it would be awfully awkward. I hope you understand?"

"Perfectly." Clarence spread a piece of toast with an immense quantity of butter. "But why should you imagine that I'd waste my young life on a third-rate line regiment?"

Manfred winced.

"You see, my son," Clarence went on deliberately, "as an officer I'd have to take any jolly old regiment that was chucked at me—just as you did." Manfred winced again. "But as a private, dear boy, I have the whole blooming Army to choose from."

"You understand?" pleaded Manfred before he made his departure. "You've got such an awful tongue that I'd be scared of you—"

"Hence!" said his brother sternly, and pointed to the door.

He chuckled all that day good-naturedly, for they were nice brothers, especially William Orlando, who wrote him from Guernsey where he was stationed. The note paper was headed "3rd Doncaster Regiment." and after opening formalities went on:

"I am awfully sick about your being ploughed at Sandhurst. Why not enlist in a good line regiment? You would be pretty sure to get a commission. Perhaps you would do better if you didn't join my regiment because it would be jolly embarrassing if you started cheeking me—"

Clarence put the letter down and laughed, for he had a very keen sense of humour. He laughed for a long time till the louder note sank into a low soft chuckle of sheer enjoyment.

Then he stopped suddenly and sat up thinking hard. He reached out his hand and took a pad of paper and a pencil from his desk, and in his round schoolboy hand he wrote:

"Major George Cassidy, 18th Rifles.

"Captain Manfred Cassidy, Royal Irish Light Infantry.

"Lieutenant William Orlando Cassidy, 3rd Doncaster."

He looked long and thoughtfully at his effort, then he rang the bell for his valet.

"Gathercole," said Clarence to the solemn-faced servitor, "we are on the verge of war."

"Indeed, sir?" said Gathercole, polite, but not greatly interested.

"Indeed," Clarence assured him. "As you know, Gathercole, I am an authority on such matters."

"Yes, sir, I am aware," responded Gathercole, with a little inclination.

"War with Germany," added Clarence unnecessarily. "In which event, the Government will need my services."

"Very naturally, sir," said the agreeable Gathercole, in a tone which implied the absurdity of conducting any war without consulting his employer.

"I shall join the Army," Clarence went on, and Gathercole nodded again. "Other men might join the Navy, but the traditions of my family demand that I should identify myself with the military organisation of the country. I shall join," he added, "as a private."

"A what, sir?" gasped Gathercole, startled out of his reserve.

"I shall join as a private," repeated Clarence firmly.

"But, you will pardon me, sir," protested Gathercole, "isn't that rather low?"

"Very," said Clarence. "It is a painful subject, Gathercole, and we will not discuss it. Is the manicurist person below? If he is, let him come up."

An hour later, Clarence Cassidy, beautiful to behold, stepped from the portals of Jermyn House into his stunningly lacquered little two-seater. His spruce chauffeur swung himself into the dicky seat and Clarence headed for the War Office.

Now the War Office, as everybody knows, is the most jealously guarded public building in London. It is as though heads of departments imagine themselves the subject of some deadly vendetta, and that it is "in the public interest" (to employ a curious figure of speech in vogue in that circle) that any request to see one man should be artfully met by producing another.

Clarence asked to see Lord Vanniker because he knew the Under Secretary of State for War slightly.

"Lord Vanniker, sir?" demanded the dumbfounded messenger. "Have you an appointment?"

"No," said Clarence, "but I hope to have."

True to its traditions, the War Office sent first a junior clerk, then a D.A.A.-G. (which means Deputy Assistant Adjutant-General). But at length Clarence, rejecting all substitutes, was ushered into the office of a real general, and finally came to the presence of his lordship, who scowled at him through a black-rimmed monocle, and asked him as plainly as it was possible to ask a man, what the devil he meant by pushing his way into the Holy of Holies of the Public Services.

"Cassidy?" The Under Secretary read the card. "I think I remember. Your father was the late Colonel Cassidy, was he not? What can I do for you, Mr. Cassidy?"

Clarence, sitting easily in the padded chair by the side of the great man's desk, pushed aside a heap of highly important documents with his elbow, and crossed his legs.

"The fact is, sir," he said, speaking slowly and deliberately, "I saw you less on my own behalf than on behalf of my brothers. Many years ago my father spoke to me of you and told me that if I was ever in a hole to go to you."

"Your father?" said the other quickly. "Not Tynemouth Cassidy?"

Clarence nodded, and the hard face of Lord Vanniker relaxed.

"Your father was one of my dearest friends," he said. "Anything I can do for you, providing of course that it is not contrary to the public interest—"

Thereafter Clarence sat and argued and pleaded for the greater part of half-an-hour.

That night he dressed himself with unusual care, rejecting waistcoat after waistcoat until, a quietly radiant being, he stepped into his car and was whirled off to Hereford Square Gardens.

"She" was a beautiful lady. Dark and clean-featured. A little imperious was she, with a trick of raising her perfect eyebrows in such a way that you might not tell where contempt and amusement began and finished.

She looked approvingly at Clarence as he came into the tiny drawing-room.

"To the minute," she drawled, with a glance at a little French clock. "You are really a very nice boy."

"Something like that has been said about me before," murmured Clarence.

"And how are all your brethren?" she smiled.

"They are pursuing their military avocations with that curious disregard for externals which is the characteristic of my house."

She laughed, and just then her serving-maid announced dinner. Over that meal he spoke of his visit to the War Office, and she was interested.

Lady Sybil Vanniker held a unique position in London Society. She knew people and, she did things. She knew, for instance, that her father, as Under Secretary of State for War, liked to be regarded as a martinet, whereas he was only a fussy old gentleman who hated anybody else to be fussy, and lived in terror lest his daughter communicated to the public press—as she had threatened to do—the fact that he smoked shag in a clay pipe—a vulgar practice carried on behind the locked door of his study.

She listened attentively whilst he described his interview with her father.

"A regiment of sharpshooters?" she repeated, and he nodded.

"A ripping idea," said he firmly, "to have nothing but the very best shots from every regiment—all jolly fine marksmen. It would be invaluable. It doesn't matter whether you take 'em from the regular army or from the territorials so long as you get 'em. See what a wonderful asset it would be to a General to have a regiment which he could use in any old place with the certainty that they could pot off any of the poor dears who stuck their silly noddles up to see what was happening."

She looked at him through her long lashes.

"Sometimes," she said, "I think you are almost clever. When did this brilliant idea strike you?"

"This morning," said Clarence. And added suddenly: "I often think of things in the morning."

It was nearly a week later that Major George Cassidy came to town in a state of great excitement. He sought out his brother to tell him the joyful news.

"A regiment of sharpshooters! Perfectly splendid idea! Did you see it in the papers? I am to be second-in-command, my boy."

Clarence let him babble on.

"I suppose it's because I'm so keen on musketry," the Major said thoughtfully. "It's rather wonderful how the War Office comes to hear of these things."

Manfred arrived late that night and broke in upon the little supper party which George was giving in honour of his appointment.

"What the dickens—?" demanded an astounded George. "I thought you were in Ireland."

Manfred smiled mysteriously.

"Brought back by telegram," he said tersely. "The fact is I've got some jolly good news to give you boys. I've been appointed to a company in the new sharpshooters' battalion."

George rose solemnly and extended his big hand.

"I'm to be second-in-command," he said. "Manfred, I congratulate you on your luck to have a chap like me to look after you."

Yet for all the hilarity there was a certain restraint between the three when they met for lunch the next day, for George and his brother had learnt from the War Office that a third officer to their corps, now mobilising at Aldershot, was Lieutenant William Orlando Cassidy.

"It's very rum," said George. "What do you think about it, Mary Ann?"

"Dear old officer," answered Clarence sententiously, "nothing is rum in this world."

Manfred regarded him solemnly.

"I think I can explain," he said with a knowing smile. "Vanniker was a great pal of the dear old governor's."

"What makes you think that?" demanded George with interest.

Manfred took a letter from his pocket and handed it over.

"Invitation to call at Hereford Square Gardens to tea," he said briefly.

The two exchanged meaning glances.

"By Jove!" said George.

At five o'clock that afternoon two perfectly groomed officers of infantry, in their neatest Aide-de-Camp-to-the-General khaki, sat decorously in the drawing-room at Hereford Square Gardens endeavouring to combine reverence for an Under Secretary of State for War with very human admiration for his beautiful daughter—a trying process demanding that the faces of the young men should be so contorted that the sides nearest the lady should smirk, and the sides presented to the War Lord should bear the stern but thoughtful expression which is demanded from military gentlemen appointed to high commands.

"You have been most kind, sir," said George at parting—earnestness and gratitude to the right—"and you also, Lady Sybil, for your interest"—tenderness and admiration to the left.

"Not at all," said Lord Vanniker gruffly. "I thought the idea of the corps an excellent one. Heartily approved throughout the Service! Wonder nobody thought of it before!" He spoke that way in his official moments.

"There is one thing, sir, that I should like to ask you." George, loyal soul that he was, braced himself for the effort. "I have a brother, Clarence Cassidy, whom you may remember."

Lord Vanniker nodded, and a little gleam of fun came into Lady Sybil's eyes.

"I was thinking, sir," stammered George, very red; "that possibly if he joined a line regiment he might in time get a commission. Not in the Sharpshooters!" he added hastily. "He's an awfully bright boy."

"Very," said Lord Vanniker with a cough, and glanced at his daughter for a lead. "Er—it was his idea."

"Sir?" said the puzzled George.

"His idea," repeated his lordship, "practically he was responsible for the corps, and he's in it."

"In it?" gasped Manfred. "A commission, sir?"

"Private," said the Under Secretary.

"He was the first to join," said Lady Sybil sweetly. "It will be awfully nice for you all—serving in the same regiment— don't you think?"

Manfred favoured her with a ghastly grin which was intended to be pleasant. He knew his Clarence!

Chapter II

The Woman of Mons

Private Clarence Cassidy, untouched and unsoiled by the dust of the long and weary road, displaying even a certain elegance in his tidy shoes, and a greater brilliance in the polished badge of his cap, sat outside the Café Rubens under the striped awning and watched the hurry and bustle of the Grande Place of Mons— that stormy city of Hainault—with a certain pleasurable sense of comfort and security which comes only to the soldier newly released from duty, having in his pocket the wherewithal to supply himself with the creature comforts which a man of leisure desires.

A tiny cup of coffee and cream was at his elbow, a half-finished petit verre of Cognac testified to his intemperance and to his contempt for Army orders, whilst a pad of paper, six sheets of which had been closely written upon, showed his criminal mind for what it was. For Clarence, despite all instructions and high commands, had given a long and very faithful account of his voyage and trials, and had made no attempt either to disguise the localities through which he had passed or to conceal the disposition of His Majesty's forces.

Two months before this story opens, Clarence Cassidy had received some disinterested advice from his three elder brothers. They had advised him—since Sandhurst had been unkind—to enlist. And each and every one of these brothers, representing three separate and distinct regiments of foot, had added an earnest rider that Clarence should choose any other regiment of the line than theirs, for Clarence had a tongue—an unpleasant tongue.

Therefore, there had come into existence a new corps—the Sharpshooters, made up of marksmen drawn from other regiments, for Clarence had secured an interview with the Under Secretary of State for War, and Clarence had dined with the daughter of the same Under Secretary, so that all the impression which he made at the War Office had been driven home by a daughter of whom, so they say, Lord Verriker was in some awe.

The idea was a good one—let there be no doubt of that.

"If the suggestion had been made by a dustman I should have accepted it," said his lordship. But the undoubted fact was that it was made by Clarence; Clarence the exquisite, the driver of lacquered two-seaters, the owner of an expensive flat. If it had been a dustman's suggestion. Major George Cassidy would not have been appointed second in command, or Captain Manfred Cassidy to the command of "A" Company, nor Lieutenant Orlando Cassidy to a platoon of "D" Company. Possibly Clarence himself would not have joined as a private; to the horror and amazement of his brethren, if this mythical dustman had poured into the sympathetic ears of an Under Secretary the necessity for raising a regiment of marksmen.

The Sharpshooters, as we all know, were the first regiment to march into Mons. They came in decorated with flowers, bestowed upon them by an enthusiastic peasantry, and they had marched to the north of the town and dug deep trenches out in the direction of Charleroi. Clarence had seen little of his three eminent brothers. Neither had so much as deigned to honour him with the slightest excuse to break through the rigid barrier of caste which separates the commissioned from the non-commissioned ranks.

On that hot August morning, when every nerve and muscle in Clarence Cassidy's body cried out aloud for relaxation and languid dalliance, he was in no mood to discuss the situation with his brethren. Yet who must loom before him, very hot and very menacing, but the second in command of his battalion. Clarence scowled horribly at his superior officer as the other came into his line of vision.

"I suppose I've got to get up and salute you," he grumbled, and rose stiffly.

"You may sit down," said George, and looked round a little fearfully.

It was a horrible thing for an officer to be seen speaking on equal terms with a private of his own regiment, an unprecedented thing in his own experience, and he had so far avoided the ordeal which he knew awaited him sooner or later.

"Are you going to have a drink, George?" asked Clarence, and beckoned the waiter.

"Look here, old man," said George Cassidy nervously, "you quite understand my position. I wanted to see you, and I heard that you were in the town, so I came in."

"And here you are," said Clarence. "Coffee or cognac, or a nice soft drink? You look a little apoplectic this morning; I should advise a lemon-squash."

George snorted, but allowed the long, cool drink to be placed before him.

"Look here, old boy," he said, more confidentially than ever, and losing all fear of major-generals in his frantic desire to relieve himself and his brothers from an intolerable situation, "can't you see how rotten it is for us?"

"When you say us," interrupted Clarence, "are you speaking for yourself, the Empire, or just editorially?"

"You know jolly well what I mean, Mary Ann!" said his indignant brother. "I'm speaking for Orlando and Manfred and myself. Dash it all, old chap, can't you see how rotten it is? Here are you, a private in the ranks, and here are we, three of your brothers, holding commissions and responsible billets, and here are you—"

"In the ranks," said Clarence, helpfully. "What are you going to do about it?"

"Well, you've got to go!" said the desperate George, and Clarence rose from the table with a pained and saddened expression.

"I've got to go?" he repeated. "Desert my country in her hour of need? Fie upon you—are you in the pay of the Germans, George?" he demanded outrageously.

George choked a little, cast imploring eyes to the cloudless heavens, shook his head and shrugged his shoulders, did in fact all the things that a man somewhat sparing of words might be expected to do when he found himself crossing swords with an orator.

"Besides," Clarence went on, "it's my regiment. I suggested it to the War Office; I, so to speak, am the father of the battalion."

He watched his brother as he walked across the place and turned into the Rue d'Havre, then he strolled down the Rue de Clercs to St. Waltrudis. Churches possessed an immense fascination for Clarence and never more so than now.

For the gaiety and the fun of soldiering had died down throughout the battalion to a sober appreciation of all that the fateful days ahead might hold. There was something very sinister in the calm of the countryside about Mons, something very ominous in the procession of motor-'buses that for days had been streaming through the quaint towns of Belgium with their incongruous advertisements and their bizarre destination boards. They were packed with khaki-clad soldiers and reeked with song and enthusiasm. And dusty artillery had been moving slowly along the broad boulevards and were halted in the shade which the Boulevard Dolcz afforded, the drivers dozing contentedly where space offered, the horses, nosebag on head, eating leisurely. Clarence passed into the cool interior of the cathedral and sat down before the high altar in a spirit of calm meditation.

It was so removed from all suggestion of war, this cool placid interior with its soft rose windows and its forest of delicate columns. Midway between himself and the altar a woman knelt, her head bowed, her hands, as he judged, clasped before her. She was slender and young—so he guessed, and he had a critical eye—and he found himself speculating upon her association with this monstrous struggle in which he had elected to play pawn.

A Belgian with a brother at the front, a young wife with a husband in Namur—you could hear the guns about Namur on a calm night—or, maybe, he was mistaken as to her age and she was a mother whose son—

She stood up suddenly, made a graceful genuflection toward the serene and misty altarpiece and turned.

Clarence started. He had not been mistaken as to her age. She was, indeed, little more than a child, slim and beautiful. Her face was pale, her eyes large and sorrowful. The redness of the firm, full, mouth contrasted vividly with the pallor of her cheeks.

For a moment she stood with one hand resting on the back of a prie Dieu, her eyes searching his face gravely. She frowned—a quick involuntary frown. It was a curiously intimate expression of her feeling. It gave this handsome young man in khaki the sense that his presence counted for something, if only it caused her annoyance.

She came down the aisle slowly, her eyes never leaving his. He thought at first that she was mistaking him for somebody else.

As she came abreast of him she stopped.

"You are English," she said in a low voice, and speaking without any trace of a foreign accent. "Will you please tell me where I can find your general?"

"Madame," said Clarence, "I should be delighted, but unfortunately I cannot tell you."

She frowned again, then pursed her lips, thoughtfully looking at him all the time.

Clarence was puzzled. This girl was so self-possessed, so suddenly and unexpectedly business-like, and, moreover, she took things for granted, such as his readiness to answer questions and, moreover, the all-important fact that he was a person of whom questions might be asked without any risk of impertinence.

"There is a regiment entrenched by the canal," she said deliberately; "they have a device on their caps as you have—crossed rifles—who is in command?"

For an instant a smile flickered on the lips of Clarence Cassidy.

"Major Cassidy," he said.

"Is he—" She hesitated and he waited. "Is he—important?"

It was on the tip of Clarence's tongue to give his views on the supreme unimportance of Major Cassidy both as a brother and an officer; he had it within him, indeed, to say that George was growing fat and he viewed with dismay his appointment to the chief command of the battalion—the colonel having broken his collar bone at Boulogne—but in the end he checked himself and lied, going to the other extreme.

"He is an immensely important man," he said in a hushed voice, which even the character of the building did not justify. "Possibly the most important—but I will not bother you with comparisons, mademoiselle."

She looked at him a little puzzled—by his educated accent probably—and walked slowly towards the door of the cathedral.

She did not speak again until he put on his cap in the big entry.

"Has your officer authority to shoot a spy?" she asked suddenly.

A staggering question from a young lady newly come from her devotions!

"We are rather whales on shooting spies," said Clarence.

She was puzzled again, but nodded and smiled.

"Come with me—follow me, please, because I do not wish to attract attention," she said hurriedly. She walked back through the Rue de Clercs, crossed the Grande Place, and where the Palais de Justice confronts the church of St. Elizabeth turned off suddenly into a narrow street.

To say that Private Clarence Cassidy was interested would be grossly understating his condition of excitement. These were ticklish days. The British Army was being rushed up to the frontier, Brussels was in the hands of the enemy, the French, by all report, were already fighting at Charleroi. The one puzzling element in the situation was the British Army, its number and composition. The people of Belgium knew nothing; the enemy knew less. One regiment, the Sharpshooters, a corps made up of the best shots of other regiments, old and trained soldiers, had been hastily sent forward to establish itself at Mons, but the strength and numbers of the divisions which were following none knew.

Clarence had a guilty feeling that in his breast pocket was a letter, addressed, it is true, to the daughter of an Under Secretary of State for War, giving much useful information; and, somehow, he divined that this business of espionage of which the girl spoke had to do with such matters.

She ran quickly up a narrow winding stair, opened a door and entered, Clarence following. It was a poorly furnished sitting-room—obviously a furnished apartment that one might hire in time of peace for a few francs a day. She closed the door behind him and motioned him to a chair.

"I had to speak to someone," she said breathlessly. "I knew no English soldiers, and I want to help France a little." She paused, her hand on her breast, breathing quickly, and her eyes compelling, luminous, ever fixed on his.

"I cannot tell now," she said, "whether I am being foolish. Let me explain briefly: My cousin was an officer in the French Army until he was court-martialled and exiled for striking his superior. I thought he was in China, but yesterday I saw him—here. He was confused, but he told me, for he is fond of me," she faltered a little, "that he knew everything about the British—where they were, the number of guns, the composition of the brigades. Perhaps, he was lying, but if he is not—I want him shot!"

She jerked herself erect as she said this, and stood, her chin pushed out, her head held high, her fine lips set firmly.

"An excellent idea," said Clarence admiringly, "and I should be perfectly charmed to oblige you, but, unfortunately, I have left my gun at home."

Again that puzzled look. She could not penetrate the atmosphere of this strange soldier, and showed herself baffled.

"But," she went on, "I want to know whether he is lying. He says that you have four divisions at Boulogne—that you have no heavy artillery."

"A lie," said Clarence gaily. He was, indeed, immensely pleased with himself of a sudden. "But the fellow you want to see, dear mademoiselle, is my chief; he'll put you right in a jiffy." He looked at his wrist watch. George would he lunching at the Grand Café.

"Come along," said he briskly, and led the way to the street, talking volubly all the time. She would have put aside the trivialities which he poured forth in an endless stream, but he gave her no chance.

George, by good fortune, was at a small table by himself.

At so unexpected a vision as a smart private of his corps accompanied by an indubitably beautiful lady, George's sentiments were of a conflicting nature.

"This lady wishes to see you, sir," said Clarence, saluting stiffly.

George bowed and went red.

"Won't you sit down—have you lunched?" he stammered. With a gracious little inclination she took a chair. Clarence remained most regimentally rigid, and George and the girl looked at him. In the lady's eyes all the tenderness of entreaty was gone. All the soft helplessness which had been directed in appeal had vanished, and in its stead he saw a cold, curious stare.

"Well?" asked George gruffly.

"The lady has a very important communication to make, sir," said Clarence.

"Thank you," growled his superior, but Clarence waited.

"You didn't ask me to stay to lunch, sir, did you?" he asked.

"I did not."

Clarence saluted and went outside to one of the many tables filled at this hour with the apprehensive burghers of Hainault.

He was the object of curiosity, but less than he had been before the motor-'buses with their khaki passengers and their dusty artillery had come.

An officer passed, walking briskly. Top-booted, scarlet breeched, with two bands of gold on his blue képi; Clarence recognised him, and rose with a salute.

The officer checked his walk and came back smiling.

"Hullo, Clarence!" he said, offering his hand. "I haven't seen you since we met at Monte Carlo!"

Baron Henthal, Intelligence Officer, Belgian Army, knew Clarence because everybody who goes to the right places at the right season knew him.

"I heard you were here—you're the chief spy catcher, aren't you?" asked Clarence curiously.

The Baron smiled.

"I am on the Intelligence Department," he said grimly, and then frowned. "It's a rotten job," he went on. "The Germans have got their best people in Belgium. I'll bet there are half-a-dozen watching us now. The men are easy to catch, but the infernal women, and especially Madeline—"

Clarence nodded:

"Madeline," he said abstractedly, "is the lady who finds things out by saying she knows something altogether different, isn't she? Tells the callow officer that there are two batteries on the road and he, poor mug, dashes in to assure her that there are three. She mentions the fact casually that she has an uncle in the Buffs, and he assures her that she means the West Kents, because the Buffs haven't come out."

The Baron eyed him keenly.

"How do you know all this?" he said. "You've described the woman perfectly."

"So long, old bird," said Clarence, ignoring the question. "Don't stand about in the sun or you'll get a headache."

"But—"

"Wait an' see," said Clarence, and sent a puzzled intelligence officer about his business.

Clarence waited, discussing a modest roll and butter and a sandwich, for the greater part of two hours. At the end of that time came George and his guest. George benevolent and grotesquely fatherly, the girl more clinging, more helpless than ever.

Swiftly Clarence stepped out and followed them as they crossed the place.

"Excuse me, sir."

George turned.

"Well?" he asked mildly.

"May I be permitted, within the provision of the Army Act, to ask whether you have soothed this lady's apprehensions?" asked Private Clarence respectfully, but with unnecessary verbosity.

His brother smiled.

"I think I may say," he said a little smugly, "that the lady has been unduly alarmed. Patriotism and all that sort of thing, Clarence. Fortunately," he nodded approvingly, "there is no fear of your being indiscreet, so the matter need not go any further. Her brother—"

"Cousin!" corrected Clarence.

"It was my brother," said the girl quickly. "I told you he was my cousin because I did not wish to—to—" She appeared to be on the verge of a breakdown and Major Cassidy scowled horribly at his imperturbable relative.

"I wish to Heaven you'd shut up, Mary Ann," he said irritably, "stickin' your infernal nose into things— anyway, her brother has been trying to frighten her."

"I see," murmured Clarence, "so it isn't four brigades we have but two—not thirty batteries of artillery, but fifteen?"

"Exactly," began George.

"No heavy guns—no wireless section—no reserve division in France yet a while," continued Clarence, with a far-away look, "only a couple of divisions of infantry, a poor old pontoon company of R. E., four regiments of cavalry—"

For a moment the eyes of the men met and George went pale. The girl looked from one to the other in apprehension. Then she turned in a flash and ran. In two strides Clarence had caught up with her and grasped her arm. He came back to his brother.

"Juggins!" he murmured. "Oh, inestimable Juggins!"

Two days later whilst the most trusted spy of the Great General Staff was using language most unbecoming in a lady, as she sat in her cell overlooking—but for frosted glass—the Boulevard des Prisons and listened to the crash of British artillery hammering at the German advance, Clarence crouching in his shelter trench by the centre canal, was pouring sotto voce comments on his superior in that superior's ear.

"You'll never be a general, sir," he hissed, as he pulled back the bolt of his Lee Enfield and thrust another clip of cartridges into the magazine. "Not in a thousand years, sir, unless you listen to your little brother. Couldn't you see she was pumping you? I saw it in a minute."

"We're not all so jolly clever as you!" growled George.

"You never spoke a truer word in your life," said Private Cassidy, and added to the man on his right:

" Sergeant Gathercole, are you trying to shoot Zeppelins?"

"No, sir," answered the sergeant.

"Then aim a little lower, you silly ass!" said Private Cassidy.

Chapter III

The Return of the Great Unwanted

Private Clarence Cassidy was doubtless a trial to his good brethren. It was not so much that they were his superiors, holding as they did commissions in His Majesty's Army, whilst he was but a humble private soldier, but that he steadfastly refused to be humble.

Brothers have served before in the same regiment, one in the place of power and the other in the ranks, but the situation has not been embarrassing to either. Clarence was respectful enough—far too respectful, he would salute and click his heels on the slightest provocation. He was punctiliousness itself with his "Yes, sirs," and "No, sirs "; he was obedient and enterprising, shirked no hardship, and asked for no favours. He was, as his own officer said again and again, all a young soldier should be and more, only—

"It is his awful tongue!" groaned Major George Cassidy to sympathetic brother Manfred. "And he gives me cheek when nobody else is around. If we could only get the young devil sent home!"

"Why not post, him to the new battalion they're forming in England?" suggested Manfred.

George's face lit up.

"That's an idea, by Jove!" said he, and sent for Private Clarence.

Clarence came—he was sleeping on the side of the road where the regiment was resting when the summons reached him—and saluted with due formality.

Far away on the right came the dull boom of guns, and overhead in the speckless blue a grey bi-plane buzzed angrily. Clarence stood blinking sleepily in the sunlight, and there was an ominous gleam in his weary eyes that warned George he must be at once brief and overpowering.

"Clarence," he said gruffly, "I've had an application this morning for instructors for the new battalion forming at Aldershot. I'm sending you home—"

"Oh, you are, are you?" interrupted Clarence, with a wicked grin. "And who the blazes told you I could instruct anybody in anything?"

"Now, look here, Mary Ann, old boy," put in the conciliatory Manfred, "there's no need to rag George. Dash it, you oughtn't to speak like that to your C.O., and—"

"You shut up, Manfred," snarled the young man, "and don't call me Mary Ann. You're setting the men a bad example. I'm not going home, and if you start any of that funny business with me I'll desert and join the Germans. After all," he said complacently, "they want a bright strategist or two."

George gasped—he took things very literally and had no sense of humour.

"Your King and your country want you," he said feebly.

"Don't talk as though you were a recruiting poster, George," retorted his younger brother sternly. "Try to realise what a tower of strength I am to the battalion. Remember how I saved you from making an ass of yourself at Mons; recall what I might in all modesty term my peerless strategy at Ham. Who saved you from getting into the wrong trenches at Le Catcau where the devils had you enfiladed and all that? Little brother Clarence!"

George looked appealingly at the handsome youth, brick red of face and shockingly soiled of garb as he was, but Clarence countered the appeal with a cold and unresponsive stare.

"We shall never get rid of the beggar," said George mournfully, after his younger brother, with a vitriolic expression of his views on people who interrupted his sleep, had returned to doze away the hours of rest.

"The best thing to do," said Manfred, profoundly, "is to see what happens."

It was the kind of thing that Manfred was always saying. He was to see "what happened" in a very little time, for even as the sharpshooters dozed, cuddling their rifles, events of some moment were going forward on their left. The 31st (Duke of Kents) Dragoons saw a chance of "pushing in" a too adventurous regiment of Prussians which was deploying across a beautifully open space in defiance of all the laws which govern the tactical offensive.

Sambrey, Colonel of the 31st, a lean and gaunt man, whipped out his sword and sent his charger spinning round to the massed squadrons.

"Thirty-first!" he bellowed. "There is your enemy! Trot! . . . Gallop! . . . Charge!"

Some say that Sambrey, who had hunted Galway regularly for thirty years, and was possessed of a fine eye for country, should have spotted the wire, but the best accounts tally in one respect, namely, that the wire was so artfully concealed that even a trained cavalry officer might be forgiven for his error. Whether the ground scouts had failed in their job will never be known, for they are now dead.

If the Colonel missed the wire, he missed the sunk road, and missed, too, the 8th Brigade of the German Army which held that road. As for the Prussian regiment in the open, that was the bait for the cavalry, and the 31st fell into the trap. Concentrated machine gun and rifle fire sent the 31st into little confused heaps of men and horses struggling on the ground.

"Cavalry charge gone wrong, I think!" said the officer commanding the Sharpshooters watching the proceedings from a gentle rise to the south. "Double forward 'A' and 'B' Companies! Orlando, take the bank of the main road and see what you can do to hold up the enemy till the cavalry get out of their trouble."

Two companies of the Sharpshooters went streaming back along the road, and you heard the clicking of their rifle bolts as they loaded at a run.

The cavalry had reformed and was coming back in open order without any apparent haste. It was not the same regiment that went into action, and in place of the gallant Sambrey there rode at its side, giving the necessary orders, a subaltern officer—the only man of commissioned rank who had escaped whole from that inferno.

A brigade of German infantry had sprung up out of the earth, and was advancing steadily across the ground which was now encumbered by the dead and the dying.

Major George Cassidy looked round at the placid landscape.

"Guns, tor the love of heaven!" he said. And as if in answer to his prayer, from a wood on the right came in rapid succession six quick stabbing pencils of flame and six cracking, crashing explosions.

Over the advancing German infantry the shrapnel burst with extraordinary accuracy. Puffy white balls of whirling smoke appeared in the heavens—"Bong! Bong!"

At the same time a heavy battery on the British left and well out of sight came into action, and the Prussian advance checked.

"Bring the left half-battalion up," said George to his adjutant brother. "We can hold these beggars till the cows come home." It was not the heroic language which is associated in the popular mind with warfare, but it was expressive and fulfilled the immediate requirements of those concerned.

Later the Anchesters and the Wigshires came up, swearing fearfully, for they had been disturbed in the midst of their dinners.

"These infernal Sharpshooters are always getting in a mess," growled the officer commanding the Wigshires. "It's the worst of having fancy soldiers on active service."

He was to discover that the Sharpshooters had no responsibility for the minor disaster which had overtaken British arms, but that did not alter his opinion of "fancy regiments" and their inutility; though, in justice, he might have admitted that the Sharpshooters were trained and picked men chosen from regular regiments for their marksmanship, and had fought a successful rearguard action for eight days, holding up the enveloping horns of von Kluck's two Army Corps.

There were other facts concerning the Sharpshooters which he could not be expected to know. The first of these was that it owed its existence to the energy and enterprise of one Private Clarence Cassidy, who, having been ploughed at Sandhurst, was urged by his military brethren (there were three, George, Manfred, and Orlando) to enlist and endeavour from humble beginnings to secure a commission in some regiment—any regiment, in fact, save those gallant corps in which the brothers were serving. For none of them had any desire to be saddled with the responsibility of Clarence-with-the-bitter-tongue.

Clarence, in a spirit of cheery malice, had driven his little two-seater to the War Office and had presented himself, immaculate and imposing, to an Under-Secretary of State for War, and had advanced his great idea—namely, that a new corps should be formed composed of marksmen drawn from other regiments; and, with the powerful aid of the Under-Secretary's daughter, had secured the appointment of his three brothers to the new regiment. Then he himself bad enlisted as a private.

That in brief is the secret history of the Sharpshooters, which had already two full-sized battles to its credit. If there were an inner ring of history Private Clarence, bandaging his little finger with great care and thoughtfulness, might have supplied the needful chapters.

Major George Cassidy, hurrying along the road, stopped before his brother.

"Hurt?" he asked.

"Desperately wounded, sir," replied Clarence cheerfully, "in the heroic performance of duty. Any reference you can make to me in dispatches would be greatly appreciated."

The Major continued his walk with a queer look on his homely face. He made a rapid survey of his line and found it good; then he went in search of his brethren. He found Captain Manfred Cassidy at the right of the line.

"Clarence is wounded," he said almost joyously.

Manfred was startled—no less was Lieutenant Orlando Cassidy, but George in a brief sentence allayed their anxiety.

The Germans, driven back by the new British force which had arrived left and right of the position, moved obliquely to the right rear, and the Sharpshooters had a moment to count noses.

A staff officer whizzed along the paved road in his car and flung a word of commendation and inquiry.

"Well done, sir! Bury your dead and get your wounded to the rear, the enemy is concentrating for another attack."

George Cassidy sought the Medical Officer attached to the regiment and poured into his ear the particulars of a great plot.

"Certainly," said the Medical Officer, wiping the perspiration from his brow with a bare arm—he was a busy man that morning, "he can look after the worst cases. I'll have the ambulance waggons up in ten minutes."

It was half-an-hour before the ambulances came.

"M.O. wants to see you, Cassidy," said a sergeant, and Clarence, sitting on the side of the road oiling the bolt of his rifle, looked up in astonishment.

"Me?" he asked incredulously.

"You. Skip lively."

Clarence walked to the dressing station, a prey to various emotions.

"Let me see that finger of yours," said the Medical Officer.

"Which finger would you like to see, sir?" asked Clarence politely.

For answer the Medical Officer caught the hand with the bandaged digit and dexterously unrolled and exposed the injury. A ricochetting Mauser bullet had taken a small piece of flesh away—as much perhaps as a clumsily handled clasp knife would have done.

The surgeon looked at the wound, and Clarence eyed the surgeon suspiciously and resentfully.

"Very serious!" said the doctor, and his voice was solemn.

"Sir," said Clarence, "when I write home I will tell my friends how your humour enlivened my hours of suffering."

The doctor, who knew his Clarence and had, indeed, been his guest on more occasions than one at some of the dainty dinner-parties Clarence was wont to give in his Jermyn Street flat, motioned to an orderly.

"Bring me a dressing—strongly antiseptic," he said.

"Why not amputate?" suggested an exasperated Clarence.

Captain Griersin, of the Royal Army Medical Corps, shook his head.

"Clarence," he said soberly, "you have an infection, my poor boy. I shall have to send you to the base."

Wrath, astonishment and amusement struggled for mastery in the face of Clarence Cassidy.

"Of all the dirty tricks!" he gasped. "Griersin, you're no sportsman!"

George, a little shamefaced but obviously relieved, came to the motor ambulance to say good-bye. He was more relieved when he found his brother in a perfectly resigned mood.

"You'll soon be back with us," he soothed.

"Your smug sympathy makes my finger ache," said Clarence testily.

"You'll be back," said .George ecstatically, "before you know where you are."

"I shall be back," said Clarence with a certain grimness, "before you know where you are!" The ambulance rolled off, leaving three officers of the Sharpshooters looking extremely thoughtful.

To illustrate adequately the further adventures of Clarence would require a large scale map of the north of France, the confidential report of General von Kluck, and the sworn statement of Lieutenant Hermann von der Grotz. As to the map, it may be said that the main road from a point south of Cambrai to the base hospital was not at the moment available for ambulance work. There were certain bridges which the British had prepared for demolition, and some which as a precautionary measure had been blown up.

The driver of the motor ambulance, who in piping times of peace had driven a Cricklewood 'bus, essayed, with the easy confidence of a Londoner, to take a short cut. As a short cut to the base hospital situated some miles in the rear, it was a ghastly failure, but as a short cut to the headquarters of the 9th Corps of the German Army it had its points.

Clarence, sitting in the rear of the ambulance, dozing in the gathering darkness and wondering sleepily where on earth the base of the army could be, heard a guttural challenge, and felt the jar of brakes.

His mind worked swiftly. He knew that the ambulance waggon would be allowed to proceed, but that any of its occupants as lightly wounded us he was would be detained. If he escaped the suspicion that he was a spy, he would certainly be made a prisoner.

He slipped off the rear seat of the ambulance, and glanced cautiously left and right. The car was in a cut road, on either side were stiff banks, and on the crest to the left he saw a shadowy group, and caught in the dusk the glint of bayonets.

Clarence understood and spoke German very well; his earlier education had been received in Heidelberg, and he had no difficulty in following the conversation which was going on between the officer ahead of the car and the sergeant of the R.A.M.C. who sat by the driver.

"We will search the car," the officer was saying, "and you may take your badly wounded on—the others will be taken out."

That was quite enough for Clarence. Crouching low, he edged to the side of the road. He scaled the bank and brought his head cautiously to the level of the edge. For a while he could see nothing, for he was looking down a slope lightly planted with trees to a dark depression, in which two fires indicated their presence by an occasional flicker of flame which leapt higher than the canvas screen which surrounded it.

Noiselessly Clarence drew himself up and rolled over to the slope. There was no sign of a sentry, and he guessed that the unconscious ambulance driver had penetrated further into the German lines than he knew. Probably the Red Cross on the hood of the car had been taken by the enemy for the mark of one of their own ambulance parties.

Clarence went forward cautiously. He avoided the depression, for in addition to the fires there were voices and a constant thud of hoofs coming and going. The road ran due east and west, so much he discovered by consulting his luminous compass.

Throughout that night he moved, as far as he could judge, in the direction of the French lines. Somewhere in the west the 8th Reserve Corps was holding the line of the Somme, and if he could only reach the rear of the German force attacking he might find a way through.

An hour before dawn he had a narrow escape. Coming slap upon a bivouac he was challenged, but fortunately for him the challenge was answered by a German officer, who must have been walking parallel to him.

The bivouac puzzled him. He was able to discern a large number of motor-cars, waggons, and portable forges packed at the side of the road.

He had no time to investigate. Dawn was too near, and already the Eastern sky was grey. He must find a dug-out in which to spend the day. He was turning sharply away, to leave the bivouac on his left, when he heard voices coming towards him.

He crouched down, pressing himself closely to the earth.

They were walking slowly toward him, three men, and they halted not more than a dozen paces from him. From the sharp gruff precision of the German he knew them to be Prussians—and officers.

"I will send out a party to bring the machine in if you think it is necessary, Lieutenant," said one, and the others made little noises of protest.

"It is not necessary, Herr Major," said one. "I purposely dropped outside of the park. If Under-Lieutenant Wessels will start the propeller... clear run across the park... no assistance."

The Major grunted his assent.

"Good luck!" he said. "Remember what you have to discover is... French reserve ... Compiègne... the forest."

Clarence listened and pieced together the purport of conversation. These men were German aviators, he gathered, and they were going out on an early morning reconnaissance. Also, this bivouac, which had puzzled him, was the Flying Headquarters of the 9th Corps.

Presently the group split up, one officer returning in the direction of the bivouac, the other two, after standing stiffly for a moment in salute, turning to the west.

Clarence followed in their wake, as noiseless as a cat. They came to a fringe of trees, which he was to discover marked the boundary wall of a big château, and passing through a broken gate, they disappeared. Clarence came after, and caught up with them, still keeping a dozen paces in the rear.

The light was growing, and by the time they reached the big monoplane, objects were visible a quarter of a mile away.

"Hurry," said the senior of the two officers, as he clambered into the pilot's seat. "Put your coat and revolver belt in the machine—the engine works stiffly."

"How am I to get in?" asked the other dubiously.

"Make a jump for it, as the machine moves forward. Quickly!"

Twice—thrice did the panting young officer pull the propeller over without result. He made a supreme effort, sending the great wooden blades spinning. With a roar the engine fired, and the propeller vanished in a circular haze.

"Now," shouted the pilot, as the monoplane jerked forward, increasing its speed with every second.

The officer who had been called Wessels ran clumsily to the side of the machine, ducking under the outspread wings of the "Taube." A moment later the bony fist of Private Clarence Cassidy shot out and caught him under the jaw.

With a leap Clarence swung himself into the frail body of the machine.

"All right," he shouted in German, and the pilot put his elevators for the climb.

In a minute they were circling above the park, Clarence utilising the time to struggle into the fur-lined coat which Lieutenant Wessels had obligingly left for him, and making himself acquainted with the lethal possibilities of that young gentleman's revolver.

For a quarter of an hour the pilot said nothing, being too busy with the purely mechanical side of aviation.

"We go due west," he shouted over his shoulder.

"North-west, I think," said Clarence.

The pilot jerked his head round at the sound of the strange voice, and faced the unsympathetic muzzle of a revolver.

"North-west and a point north," said Clarence gently, "or I shall blow the top of your head off, Herr Lieutenant."

Major George Manfred had given the order to "stand to" with the coming of dawn, and the Sharpshooters, weary and grimy, were lining the trenches into which they had struggled the night before.

"I'm jolly glad Clarence is out of this," he was remarking to his brother when:

"Mark over, sir!" yelled a peculiarly dirty subaltern. "Taube on the right makin' for these lines... Platoon... volley firing... Ready... Present... Fire... Got it, I think, sir?"

Got it, indeed, for the Taube lurched like a wounded bird, and came settling in short, impatient circles before the trenches!

The men scrambled out to greet a very angry young observer.

"Dash it, sir," he said, "you jolly nearly killed me—and you've smashed my steering apparatus!"

"Clarence!" gasped George.

"Clarence it is, sir!" said that young man, stretching his stiff limbs and grinning pleasantly at a scowling young officer of the German Air Service.

Major George said nothing for a while, then:

"Mary Ann," he remarked solemnly, "nothing will kill you—you're like a cat."

"Yes, sir," said Clarence briskly, "the cat that has the disgusting habit of coming back."

Chapter IV

The Losing of the Orlando

The guns were talking incessantly around by Ciry Wood. An angry chatter of machine guns had followed the inquisitive intrusion of two companies of Sharpshooters.

"See what you can find in Ciry Wood," the brigadier had said, and the Sharpshooters had found machine guns. There was no need to make any very close inspection to reveal their presence. Crouching in the shelter of a Heaven-provided sunk road, the Sharpshooters listened to the infernal p-wish! of flying bullets with interest, but without enthusiasm.

"There's a brigade in front of us," said Lieutenant Orlando Cassidy in a fret. "They are working round to the right, too."

His whistle shrilled.

"Company will retire—platoon commanders get your men across that beet field and dig in to the left of that white house."

"May I respectfully suggest, sir," murmured a voice in his ear, "that we remain in our present position until we see what plans our jolly old General has?"

Orlando Cassidy wrinkled his nose in a grimace.

"For the Lord's sake, Clarence, let me run this show!" he begged. And Clarence, private and brother, shrugged his shoulders.

"Our blood be on your head," he said ominously.

How the company crossed the field under a fire which has been variously described as "withering" "deadly" and "devastating" has been told. How it dug itself in on a position which was exposed to heavy shell and machine-gun fire, and how it was eventually rescued from its precarious position by a brilliant bayonet charge executed by "A," "C," and "D" companies of the Sharpshooters, aided by Private Clarence, who virtually directed the retirement, is written largely in the history of the regiment—at any rate, that history for which Clarence himself claims responsibility.

You must remember that Private Clarence Cassidy of the Sharpshooters was no ordinary private. Ordinary privates, or prospective privates, do not importune war ministers with schemes for the formation of a new regiment. Nor do they so lay their plans and urge their arguments, that a member of the Cabinet arranges for this prospective private's brothers to hold commissions in that corps, being transferred from likely regiments for the purpose.

In the ordinary course of affairs, and in consonance with the generally accepted idea of how these things should be, it is the officer who works on behalf of his less fortunate brother in the ranks and utilises his undoubted influence in order to secure his advancement. There could be little doubt that Private Clarence Cassidy caused the 1st Sharpshooters to be formed, for no other reason than to secure a position in a regiment in which his brethren held commissions. It was no strong sense of fraternity that caused him to take this step, but that mordant sense of humour which ever characterised his dealings with his less brainy brothers.

With his eldest brother, George, second in command (and lately actually commanding the regiment); with his second brother, Manfred, lording a company; and his third, Orlando, though but a subaltern officer, commanding his company also, Clarence took some joy in the knowledge that if the worse came to the worst, there would never arise any question as to his next of kin. Nor, thought he comfortably, would he ever disappear into the oblivion which sometimes awaits the man against whose name the word "missing" is appended; for, to be sure, one or the other of his relatives would be on hand to give very definite news to the world of his whereabouts.

The end of the long and trying march from Mons to the Marne found Private Cassidy with two passionate desires uppermost in his mind. The first was for a bath and a complete change of clothing; but the second had directly to do with his private conscience. In the lonely but too short watches of the night, and in the long silence of the dogged march southward, there had dawned upon him a sense of his responsibility.

One night, when the pressure had to some extent been taken off the regiment, and the Sharpshooters were billeting pleasantly in a little town north and east of Paris, Clarence was summoned to the "billet" of his superiors, and was shown into the drawing-room of the little château which was for the moment the headquarters of the battalion, where the anxious Cassidy family awaited him.

"Sorry to bother you," said George, after he had closed the door carefully, that no military ear might be shocked by this flagrant contravention of King's regulations—for your commissioned officer is not enjoined to take too keen an interest in the social welfare of his men. "But the fact is, old man, you have been looking a bit droopy this last day or two. You aren't ill, are you?"

There was a malicious gleam in Clarence's eye, as he caught the uncomfortable gaze of his elder brother.

"Are you thinking of sending me sick?" he asked.

"Good Lord, no!" protested George, with great vigour.

He had once "sent him sick," and had lived to regret it. But that is another story, and besides it has already been told.

"Mary Ann, old man," broke in Manfred, "we don't want you to get a rotten idea of us. I am willing to admit that it was a bad break on all our parts when we tried to get you to enlist in a line regiment, and did our best to keep you out of the battalions in which we were serving."

Clarence looked thoughtfully out of the window at the dusty landscape, the fires that burnt so boldly in the middle of the village street, at the constant procession of dust-stained limbers and weary horses that were passing at a snail's space to the next village and to the greatly desired "billet." He looked so long and so earnest, that they thought he had not heard what George had said; and the cautious Orlando third of the trinity of elder brethren, lank, hard, and sandy, would have called his attention to the handsome admission which Manfred had made, but that Clarence suddenly broke his silence.

"There have been bad breaks all round," he said. "It was a pretty foolish mistake for you fellows to make; but then I ought to have known, and, indeed, I did know, that all you dear chaps are horribly deficient in intelligence."

Nobody winced. They would have been wincing all day long at Clarence-with-the-bitter-tongue, if they noticed a little thing like that.

"It was my mistake entirely," Clarence went on, a little sadly. "And, of course, it was quite unpardonable of me, because, as you know, I have the brains of the family."

Nobody denied this outrageous claim; and, after another brief and gloomy survey of the darkening landscape, Clarence turned with a melancholy shake of his head to his three brothers, alert and on the defensive. They knew that something particularly unpleasant was coming.

"It was an awfully good joke for me," mused Clarence aloud, "getting you three fellows transferred to the regiment in which I was serving as a private; because I know you just hate having me anywhere round, not because you have any unnatural antipathy to me, but because it follows that the clever one of the family always shows the other chaps up."

"It was a joke," said George heartily. "We expected it, and we accept in that spirit. Now we want bygones to be bygones, Mary Ann. We'll start afresh. You'd better accept a commission and come in with us."

But Clarence, staring at him with an unresponsive eye, shook his head again.

"It's worrying me," he said, shortly.

"What is worrying you?"

"You and Manfred and Orlando," said Clarence.

George frowned.

"What the devil is there about us to worry you?" he asked irritably.

Again there was a little pause, and then Clarence spoke.

"I see where I've been wrong," he said. "It wasn't playing the game to get you in a regiment like this."

"But, my dear chap," expostulated George, "It's a jolly good regiment."

"That's what I mean," said Clarence calmly. "It's a jolly sight too good a regiment. You aren't up to the weight, George," he said gently. "Nor is Manfred, nor you, my son." He shook a reproving finger at the outraged Orlando.

There was a period of silence, and then George demanded, with ponderous sarcasm:

"May I ask what you intend to do about it?"

"I'm going to get rid of you," said Clarence.

There was a triple but unanimous gasp.

"Get rid of us?" repeated Manfred incredulously. "Is this a joke or something?"

"It's not a joke," replied Clarence; "but it is—something. I've thought it all over," he went on briskly, "and I've decided that I ought not to have endangered the lives of my comrades by placing chaps like you in a responsible position. I don't exactly know how to get rid of you all"—he looked round a little helplessly—"but it must be done."

"Now, look here, Mary Ann," began Manfred; but Clarence, with a lofty wave of his hand, arrested the eloquence of the other.

"It has to be done," he said solemnly. "What happened the day before yesterday?"

He fixed Orlando with an accusing eye, and his brother went red.

"You entrenched your men in the one place in the whole of France where the enemy could over-shoot you, enfilade you, and surround you."

"A joke's a joke!" said Orlando hotly. "I did the best I could do under the circumstances, and even the General admitted—"

"The General knew a jolly sight less about it than you did," said the calm Clarence. "You must understand that I've studied these matters. I'm a positive whale on strategy and on the technical defensive—the General didn't see what I saw. And anyway, you were out of the trenches because the other companies relieved you before the General came up. No, Orlando, you must go!"

"I think this has gone a little too far," began George.

"I don't want any of your heavy-fatherisms," snarled Clarence. "I've come to deliver my ultimatum. You can either get yourselves killed or can invalid yourselves to the base. Otherwise it will be my painful duty to remove you."

He settled his cap at a rakish angle, saluted stiffly, and was gone before they found their tongues. Then:

"Of all the impudence!" gasped George. And for the rest of the night the conversation mainly centred around Private Clarence Cassidy.

Now it is a fact that Lieutenant Orlando Cassidy, though an excellent musketry instructor, whose knowledge of the rifle and its mysteries fully justified his appointment to the Sharpshooters, had one or two distressing disadvantages from which he could not possibly hope to escape, since even war, revolutionary as it is, neither changes the leopard's spots nor brings to the face of the Ethiopian the milk and roses of the Devonian's complexion.

Orlando was one of those men who from their early youth up assumed the settled habits which are peculiar to the middle-aged. Orlando was a famous "forty-winker," one of those uncomfortable persons to whom a doze between lunch and tea is as part of a solemn ritual. Consequently there may have been some truth in the charge which Clarence promulgated, which was to the effect that Orlando had slept through a certain vicious attack of the enemy upon the Sharpshooters' line, and that an enterprising signaller, seeing his commanding officer sitting in the corner of the trench, looking somewhat unlovely with his mouth agape, had been on the point of reporting his death to Army Headquarters.

Major George Cassidy, therefore, was flying in the face of Providence when on the day following this conversation, under orders from the brigadier to provide a reconnoitering party to move in the direction of the enemy's line, he chose Lieutenant Orlando Cassidy for the service. It was more by accident than design that Private Cassidy himself accompanied this little expedition, which had as its object the seizing of a farmhouse three miles to the left of the line which was now advancing from the Marne to the Aisne, and the reporting upon the enemy's strength in that quarter.

Nobody expected a great number of Germans to be found upon that front, because about this time Von Kluck's corps was edging northward and westward toward the quarries of Soissons. But it was known that there were wandering Uhlan patrols, and that a company of Jaegers had been seen in the neighbourhood. The reconnaissance went off with little incident; a hungry German or two surrendered himself and was sent under escort to the base; but no considerable force was revealed.

"We will entrench beyond the farm," said Orlando to his junior subaltern, "and I will take a couple of men and go forward to see what I can find."

He looked round, hesitated, then beckoned Clarence and another man. He had not forgiven Clarence his insolence, and was inclined to be a little gruff. Making no further remark, he swung off along the white road, climbed through a hedge, and moved cautiously across a deep hill toward a rise on his right, which would give him as he thought an uninterrupted view of the country. He dropped the first man of his private line of communication a mile from the farm, and another mile or so beyond this he turned to Clarence:

"You stay here," he said, "and pass any signal back I give you."

"Yes, sir," answered the obedient Clarence.

"I shall be gone some time," said Orlando, and unconsciously patted his haversack, where a most excellent lunch, prepared that morning at his billet, bulked largely.

Clarence watched his brother move off, saw the khaki figure grow smaller and smaller and finally disappear in a cloud of green undergrowth. Clarence squatted down to wait. The sun was hot, but a little breeze came to him across the scented fields. The guns were far away, and only now and again came to him like the echo of distant thunder. It was curious, he thought, that war was in this pleasant land, with its white châteaux, its grass-green woods, its glimpses of silvery river. And yet that sluggish river, which sent the sunlight flashing back to him where he sat was a great barrier, to cross which thousands of men would sacrifice their lives, and to prevent that crossing thousands of others would die as cheerfully.

He shook his head in wonder at the absurdity of it all, then turned to keep his eye fixed upon the place where Orlando had disappeared. Clarence felt, rather than knew, that there was no danger in the position the company occupied; and that the chance of finding any considerable body on this front was very remote. His brother was less certain, if one could judge by the length of time he took to make his survey. Clarence guessed that Orlando was adding a little pleasure to the business of the moment, and that the excellent luncheon was in course of consumption.

He waited another half-hour, and still there was no sign of Orlando, and he began to be a little alarmed. Unless the officer had found himself unexpectedly in a position which rendered it extremely dangerous for him to move, he should be back by now.

Clarence rose, and, picking up his rifle, followed the way Orlando had gone, keeping his eyes sweeping ahead left and right for any sign of his brother's re-appearance. He reached the thicket, and had no difficulty in finding the path which Orlando—who had no original ideas, and was always prepared to tread the road which somebody else had made—had taken.

There was no sound and no sign of his officer. Clarence came cautiously to open ground, a level stretch of sward which sloped gently down to a little river and to the fringe of a tiny village. He looked around, and then he saw the missing man.

Orlando had assured himself that there was very little to see, and he had lunched, for the remains of his collation were spread upon the white napkin in which they had been wrapped, and his Thermos flask stood most improvidently uncorked by his side. As for Orlando—with his legs stretched wide apart, his arms happily folded, and a beatific smile upon his countenance—he was sleeping gently and sweetly the sleep of a man of habit, who had already accomplished a good half-day's work and is anxious to prepare himself for the second half.

Clarence looked, a big grin upon his face, and he chuckled silently.

Then a sound made him turn swiftly. Somebody was moving through the undergrowth to his left, moving stealthily and furtively, and in few seconds that somebody exposed himself to be a young, very healthy-looking Prussian officer, revolver in hand, and the butt-end of a cigar between his teeth.

He did not see Clarence quite soon enough, and the muzzle of the young man's rifle was aimed directly at his good German heart before ho realised exactly what was going forward, and he dropped his revolver on the turf at his feet and raised his hands.

"Hard luck!" he said, with a gleam of amusement in his eyes. He spoke most excellent English, with an American accent.

"Very hard luck indeed! Do you want to surrender?" asked Clarence.

"Not in the slightest," said the German officer coolly. "As a matter of fact I spotted your company at the farm and was prowling round looking for stragglers." There was a little pause.

"I am afraid that I am booked for one of your excellent concentration camps," went on the German officer. "Tough luck after coming all the way from Philadelphia to serve my country, to find myself in this unhappy predicament!"

"Devilish tough luck!" said Clarence. "But then, you see, it's all the fortune of war, and it might have been the other way round."

A thought came upon him in a flash.

"Are you very keen upon taking a prisoner?" he asked suddenly.

"I am not exactly dying to take one, but I should certainly have liked to return to my regiment with something to my credit."

Clarence grinned, and turned his head. Orlando was still asleep.

"You can have him!" he said. "But don't hurt him: he's my brother."

The German officer looked from one to the other in amazement.

"He's as quiet as a mouse," Clarence went on, tabulating the virtues of the unconscious Orlando. "He won't bite or scratch, but he'll go very quietly. He's a fastidious feeder, but otherwise wants very little."

"I will see that he gets it," said the German gravely.

"Cheer-o!" said Clarence, and held out his hand, and the alien enemy shook it heartily.

"My name is Derndoff," he said. "Look me up if you're ever in New York. Otherwise—"

He shrugged his shoulders.

"Look after him," said Clarence, and he tiptoed back down the hill. He moved a little way down and then he turned.

"I forgot to tell you," he said in a loud whisper, "that he answers to the name of Orlando."

Chapter V

The Ghost of Napoleon

Four brothers serving in one regiment are three brothers too many. This was the view held in the 1st Sharpshooters. Not, be it said, by the men themselves, not by Major George Cassidy, commanding that regiment, nor by Captain Manfred Cassidy, nor yet by Lieutenant Orlando Cassidy.

It was, however, very strongly held by Private Clarence Cassidy, who openly expressed his gratification when the news came through that Lieutenant Orlando, his good, but sleepy brother, had been captured by the enemy.

"A jolly good thing for the Army!" he said, speaking privily to his gloomy brethren.

Insubordination could go no further. The subject of Orlando's internment was a constantly recurring one, and Manfred and George enlivened many a weary hour in the trenches with a discussion which raged round the following points of perplexity:

1. Was Orlando asleep when a German officer discovered him? If so, was Orlando liable to a court-martial— for he was scouting at the time?

2. Did Private Clarence Cassidy, who was in support of his brother, hold a long conversation with the German officer who captured Orlando, as some of the men reported?

3. Was Private Cassidy responsible for the internment of Lieutenant Orlando Cassidy, being urged to action by his (Clarence's) contempt for Orlando's military qualities?

"It's a very curious thing," said Major George Cassidy ominously, and shook his head. "Very curious indeed!"

"Have you had any further news?" asked his troubled brother.

Major Cassidy nodded.

"He is a prisoner of war in one of those beastly places in Germany, and he's fairly happy; but how he was taken prisoner without Clarence knowing is a mystery to me."

Captain Manfred Cassidy speared a sardine out of a tin. He was sitting vis-à-vis with his brother in the trenches before the Aisne, and the hour was breakfast time.

"Perhaps he was asleep?" suggested Manfred.

"I do wish you wouldn't make such ridiculous suggestions," said his elder brother testily. "Of course, Orlando wasn't asleep. You know the Cassidy breed; we never sleep, Manfred."

Manfred accepted this startling claim without comment, but from somewhere down the trenches came a little happy chuckle of laughter, and George glared up.

"What is amusing you, Private Cassidy?" he asked.

Private Clarence Cassidy, leaning against the clay side of the trenches, touched his cap humbly.

"I was thinking of a joke, sir—a joke I read in Punch."

"Jokes in Punch wouldn't make you laugh like that," said Manfred suspiciously.

"That, sir," said Clarence, "is a reflection upon England's premier journal of humour, which I shall not fail to convey to the right quarter."

He was left-hand man of his company in the trench line, and his nearest companion was half-a-dozen paces off. For the Sharpshooters were holding a front which, according to all the text books, should have been held by at least two battalions. The conversation, therefore, was restricted to three men. I make this explanation lest it be thought, to Private Clarence Cassidy's discredit, that his attitude of speech and mind should be subservient to military discipline.

"Of course, he wasn't asleep!" said Major George, turning to his brother and lowering his voice a little. "It would have been a dashed unprofessional thing to do."

"You know what Orlando is," said Manfred apologetically.

"I know what our House is!" retorted George loftily. "In such a situation Orlando would have been alert and wakeful, eager for duty."

"Ha, ha!" said the scornful voice of Clarence again; but George ignored the interruption.

"Do you remember," asked Manfred slowly, "how Clarence suggested that you and I and Orlando ought to get out of the army, and how he threatened that he would jolly well get us out?"

Major George Cassidy frowned.

"I remember something about it," he said slowly.

"I wonder," Manfred went on, lowering his voice, "if there was anything in it."

"Nonsense!" said his commanding officer sharply. "You don't suggest that Clarence would go over to the enemy and arrange for them to come and take poor old Orlando prisoner, do you?"

"It was very funny," said Manfred, and that was the only statement he would permit himself to make.

Undoubtedly it was very funny, and undoubtedly Orlando was asleep, on reconnaissance duty; and less doubt is there that Private Clarence—or, as his affectionate family preferred to describe him, "Mary Ann"—had hailed a Heaven-sent German officer, himself engaged in reconnaissance work, and like a modern and unpicturesque Benjamin, Orlando had been handed over to captivity.

There was romance in the beginning of the Sharpshooters; there promised to be greater adventure in its finish, so far as the three brothers of Private Clarence Cassidy were concerned. Clarence had raised the regiment, in the sense that he had conceived the idea of a corps formed from the best shots of other battalions to be employed in pure rifle work. That he had imposed his scheme upon an Undersecretary of State for War, and had exerted his undoubted influence (for Private Clarence Cassidy before he enlisted was a young man of some importance) to induce the War Secretary, in his appointment of officers to the new corps, to choose those three brothers who had separately and severally expressed their passionate desire that Clarence should serve in any other regiment than theirs, was indeed a modern miracle. Seeing them safely attached to the regiment, Clarence had enlisted as a private, and rejecting all blandishments, continued to serve in that humble capacity.

He edged along the trench as his brothers continued their conversation in a low tone, and suddenly broke in upon them, yet without seemingly addressing them directly, for his face was turned towards that patch of country where the enemy was supposed to be and from whence at regular intervals his shells came shrieking overhead to burst in a horrid din at the rear of the trench.

"You chaps are talking about me," he said, not lowering his voice, yet pitching his conversation to such a tone that the other men could not hear him.

"We were talking about poor Orlando," said George gravely.

"Why poor?" asked Clarence, with rare insolence. "He's a jolly sight better off where he is, and so are we."

"That sounds to me like mutiny, Clarence," said George reproachfully. "When you remember what our House has done for the Empire—"

"Dear old thing!" interrupted Clarence, in a voice of pity. "I've done lots of things, not only for the Empire but for the Alhambra and the jolly old Hippodrome, but I never boast about it. And besides, what I say is quite right," he went on; "C" Company would have been carved up if old Orlando had been in charge the other day when we took that beastly river."

"I hope you will not speak disrespectfully of Orlando, Clarence. Do not forget that he is not only your officer but your brother."

Clarence made a strange barking noise which conveyed in some subtle manner his derision and disrespect.

"That's the pathetic part about it," he said. "If he hadn't been my brother I should have written to the Times about him. He can thank his lucky stars that he is my brother, and so can you chaps."

He still talked to the hills to all appearance, not so much as turning his face in the direction of his superior officers. Now and again, in the little pauses which punctuated every sentence, he trimmed his nails with great earnestness and diligence, dividing his attention between his well-kept hands and the enemy ahead.

"What have we been doing?" said Manfred, with some attempt at heavy jocularity.

"Transports," replied Clarence briefly. And at that word Manfred went very hot and squirmed. It was a sore subject, the question of the Sharpshooters' transport. The officer in charge of the waggons had gone sick on the way up to the Aisne, and in his goodness of heart Captain Manfred Cassidy had assumed the responsibilities and duties of regimental Supply officer. The Army Service Corps cannot always be nursing and attending the bleating battalions. Sometimes regiments must fend for themselves, and depend upon their own intelligence and initiative to carry with them to the firing line the munitions of war and the reserves of food which are necessary to their salvation. And Manfred had first lost his regiment and then had lost his supply waggons. That is putting it brutally and briefly, but it describes faithfully exactly what happened.

Manfred talked about wrong roads and bad directions. He even hinted that the General Staff had maliciously issued maps which were specially designed and printed to lead astray an amateur supply officer. To put the matter in a nutshell, the Sharpshooters spent one bitter day and night eating their emergency rations and cursing the regiment, whichsoever it might be, which was at that moment enjoying the bully beef and marmalade intended for the corps commanded by Major George Cassidy. The regiment in question, as it happened, was a Cockney regiment without a conscience, and with an enormous appetite; and when at last the Sharpshooters' supply waggons were sorted out from the division into which they had wrongfully strayed, they were found to be intact in every particular—save in supplies. This was a sore point with the Sharpshooters, but a much sorer point with Manfred Cassidy.

"You know jolly well, Clarence," he said, with a great attempt at sternness, yet with some fearful respect for this Clarence-with-the-bitter-tongue, which all his brothers possessed and which even remote cousins shared. "You know jolly well how the thing happened. It wasn't my fault at all."

"It was the fault of the man who made the roads," said Clarence gently. "Poor old Napoleon—put it on to him. He's dead, anyway."

Manfred relapsed into a dignified silence, but Clarence, after whistling a thoughtful stave, returned to the charge.

"I'm afraid you'll have to go, too, Manfred," he said regretfully. "I don't know how it can be managed, but I feel that somehow Providence in its mercy will show us the way."

"Do you mean to tell me—" began the wrathful George.

"I mean to tell you," said Clarence firmly, "that for the salvation of the Empire about which you were speaking so familiarly a few minutes ago, it is necessary that Manfred direct his undoubted genius to another sphere."

That night, when the Sharpshooters had been relieved by another regiment, and were moving back to their billets in a little French town west of Soissons, George and Manfred walked side by side in earnest consultation.

"If he says he'll do it, he'll do it," said Manfred miserably. "Upon my soul! I'm beginning to get scared of him, George."

"Leave everything to me," replied his elder brother confidently. "I think I know how to manage Mary Ann."

But thereafter Manfred watched his younger brother apprehensively and expectantly. Had Clarence Cassidy been an active member of the Borgia family, and Manfred one who had knowingly or unwittingly trodden upon his moral corn, the young private of the Sharpshooters could not have been an object of more constant vigilance.

Clarence was, to all outward appearance, in his meekest and most amiable mood in these days. He seldom approached his brethren except—in accordance with the King's regulations—accompanied by the inevitable non-commissioned officer; nor did he suggest by his attitude that he was laying any plot for the discomfiture of Manfred.

The way back was not a pleasant one. It lay through a country where the regiment had to make a long detour to avoid a road commanded by the enemy's batteries. The byways of France, after a week of ceaseless rain, were so many quagmires, and even the little strip of paving which centre some of these roads was little more than an obstacle.

Darkness had set in when the regiment began its march to the billets, and with the dark came a fine drizzle of rain, incessant and uncomfortable. There were convoys moving up from the firing line which had to be avoided, batteries moving forward in the night, which sent the regiment ankle-deep into the loamy fields, and dawn was coming greyly to the east when the regiment arrived at Deny, a village built about a lordly château, one wing of which was a mass of blackened flint and twisted metal, but which nevertheless offered commodious quarters to the weary and bedraggled officers of the Sharpshooters.

The Château Deny was in every sense historic. It was built upon the side of a castle which, in the days of Philip, had dominated the valley of the Aisne, and had been held by one family for close on five hundred years. This, Manfred, marching by the side of his younger brother, and with some desire to propitiate him of the vitriolic tongue, informed Private Clarence.

The present owner, said he, was one of those eccentric persons who had regarded with lofty disdain the advance of the German Army, and had remained in his château, guarding his wonderful Napoleonic relics until he had seen a portion of the house crumble to dust and flames, under the persuasive powers of a twelve-inch howitzer.

"The rum thing is," said Manfred, "that the devils should have left the château without looting it—it is simply filled with valuables."

"Then we may be able to pick up a few things," said Clarence hopefully.

There was enough to pick up, as he discovered later, when he was posted as sentry at the door of the great salon, which housed perhaps the finest private Napoleonic museum in France. For here were not only the relics of the Italian campaign—the chairs, camp-stools, the dinner services, the foot-warmers, and cocked hats of the great general—but with painstaking thoroughness the Comte Deny had had a whole series of uniforms constructed, illustrating the progress of the Little Corporal from barrack-room to Nôtre Dame.

George and Manfred, inspecting the relics, must halt at the door of the salon before a very stiff and formal sentry and talk psychology.

"The very influence of these things which have been touched and used by The Master," said George in an awed voice, "is particularly inspiring. It gives you a sort of—you know what I mean."

"Pain in the neck," murmured a suggestive voice at his elbow.

"I quite understand what you mean, sir," replied Manfred, ignoring the interruption, and punctiliously respectful. "I felt it myself. It sort of bucks you up—makes you feel as though Napoleon himself were watching you."

"He would have laughed his head off if he had watched you this last week or two," said the sentry.

"Particularly inspiring!" said George again, and, arm in arm with his brother, stalked down the corridor to the smaller salon which the officers of the Sharpshooters were using as a messroom.

Private Clarence, whose duty it was to act for the moment as custodian of these treasures, carefully locked the door and put the key in his pocket, and this, with numerous others, he handed over to his relief an hour later.

The news which came in from Divisional Headquarters that night was good. Somewhere behind the forest of Compiègne, hidden away in forest, in town, in great houses chock-a-block with men, had been the new army of the Republic which the baffled airmen of Germany had failed to discover. It had made its rendezvous upon the German right, and von Kluck, swerving away like a frightened horse in the direction of the Marne had felt his first check. He had turned, fighting desperately for the heights of the Aisne and for the barring river, which would give him an hour or two's respite from his ruthless and relentless pursuer.

A position of stalemate had been established, and weary regiments could be relieved for rest and refreshment. For the Sharpshooters, who had fought without ceasing since the days of Mons, the lull was very acceptable indeed.

"I think I shall employ my time in working up my acquaintance with Napoleon," said Manfred importantly.

In his less military moments he was inclined to be a little pompous, and his weakness lay in the direction of exceedingly dull papers, which he insisted upon reading before the Royal United Services Institute.

"I rather fancy," he reflected, "that I could write a little monograph upon the contents of this château alone."

"Which is haunted, sir," chirped a junior subaltern from the other end of the table.

"Haunted my grandmother!" said the practical George. "Pass the pickled onions."

Manfred went to bed that night with two thoughts fighting for the front rank. The first was the uncomfortable feeling which he had had, ever since the unhappy disappearance of Orlando, that Clarence-of-the-bitter-tongue, who had expressed in the frankest terms his contrition that he had ever introduced three such unadulterated duffers into the Sharpshooters, was working steadily to secure the retirement from that regiment of his elders and betters.

Of course, it was all very absurd that a commissioned officer of His Majesty's Army, with some experience in the handling of men and the solving of complex problems, should worry himself for a moment over the machinations of a private soldier of his own regiment. But then Clarence was not an ordinary private. Far more pleasant was it to turn to his second obsession, and drag it into the first place. This monograph on Napoleon would make an excellent paper to read when the war was over, might indeed become a standard monograph, or, with luck, achieve a modest circulation printed in pamphlet form in one of those unattractive covers which invariably conceal the efforts of military genius, at sixpence nett.

Not that Manfred, or any of his brothers, troubled greatly about money, because they were all well provided with this world's goods. None of them, perhaps, was quite so rich as Clarence, who enjoyed three distinct and separate incomes, but they were all fairly rich men. Still, the fact that one could sell one's work gave it a far greater importance than if one merely had it printed for private circulation and distributed it gratis to one's friends.

With these happy speculations Manfred, uttering a sigh of content, turned over in the most comfortable bed he had slept in since he left England, and fell asleep.

What woke him he could not say. It was an indescribable sound, as though a soft hand had brushed along the silken coverlet of the bed.

"Who's there?" he said quickly. But no answer came.

It was a light night, with the moon shining through the long French windows of the big bedroom. They fell aslant of a figure, half in light and half in gloom, which stood brooding at one of the windows.

Manfred's sandy hair almost stood on end. There was no mistaking that personality or that attitude. A stout figure, much taller than Manfred had thought, hands clasped behind his back, chin on his breast, his cocked hat correctly athwart his head. He would have recognised it without the ribbon of an order across the epaulletted coat, or the Hessian boots. Without the little telescope under its arm, or the dim iron sword at its side. The face was in the shadow, but Manfred seemed to trace the familiar lines of the great general. The figure turned so that its back was towards the bed, moving slowly across the room and disappeared through the portiered doorway.

For fully two minutes Manfred sat bolt upright, frozen stiff with astonishment. Then he leapt out of bed, darted through the door and fell full length over a chair which some fool had carelessly placed in the very middle of the corridor. His voice aroused the sleepers. Doors opened, electric torches flashed, and George, in his vivid pyjamas, arrived on the scene with a revolver in one hand and a candle in the other. He recognised the disturber of regimental peace instantly.

"What the devil's the matter with you, Manfred?" he asked, for fraternal affection will not survive a night alarm.

"I've seen him!" said Manfred eagerly.

"Seen who?" asked a dozen scornful voices.

"Napoleon!" said Manfred.

Twelve pairs of eyes looked from one to the other, and then, as if by common consent, stared inquiringly at their commander.

Major George Cassidy shuffled uncomfortably.

"What the deuce were you drinking last night, Manfred?"

"Nothing!" replied the indignant Manfred. "Do you think I've—"

"I think you've been dreaming," said George. "What did you see?"

Briefly Manfred narrated the story of the apparition. It was fortunate that so intelligent a person as Private Clarence Cassidy was on guard at the salon at the other end of the corridor. He had seen nothing and had heard nothing, save the hullaballoo which, he informed his commanding officer with admirable respect, was of such a character as to suggest that some of the gentlemen of the mess had been enjoying a birthday party.

This and other innuendoes, all more or less discreditable to Manfred, were passed over by George as being unworthy of notice, and the officers of the Sharpshooters retired to their interrupted clumbers.

This happened between ten and twelve o'clock at night—for soldiers are folks who go early to bed—and no further sound disturbed the harmony of the Château Deny, until a wild yell, a smothered exclamation, and a most alarming crash, called George again from his bed into the corridor.

He found Manfred slowly picking himself up and disentangling himself from a whole barricade of chairs and small tables which had been set in his path. He was neither inclined to be apologetic nor gentle. He had seen Ney!

The great marshal himself, with his red side-whiskers, had appeared exactly in the same manner as Napoleon had, and had stood brooding out upon the landscape in the half-light and shadow of the moon.

"I think you'd better go to bed," said George gently.

"I'm telling you," said the exasperated Manfred, "that I saw—"

"Yes, yes, I know," said George soothingly, and patted his brother on the back. "I'm sure what we've had to go through this last month or so is enough to upset any fellow."

With the sympathetic murmurs from his brother officers sounding in his ears, Manfred turned with a snarl to his elder brother.

"Do you suggest that I'm mad?" he said.

"No, no, no," said George. "You're all right, old man. I'm standing by you, I'll see you through. Come along to bed, dear chap, and I'll sit by your side."

"Go to the devil!" snapped Manfred, and would have made a dignified exit from the company had his stalk not been pulled up short by the slippery nature of the floor, which some mischievous miscreant had most industriously soaped in the darker hours of the morning.

"What time were you on duty on the night poor old Manfred saw the ghost?" asked Major George Cassidy sternly.

"From ten to twelve, and from four to six, sir," replied Private Clarence, regimentally erect.

George was silent for a little while.

"I suppose you knew we've sent poor old Manfred to the base for a rest cure?" he asked carelessly.

"I heard something about it, sir," said Private Clarence Cassidy.

Another pause.

"You didn't see the ghost yourself?" asked the Major.

Clarence Cassidy shrugged his shoulders.

"My dear old bird," he said, "what perfectly piffling questions you ask a chap! Of course I didn't see the ghost. Although"—he hesitated—"although I fancy I caught a reflection of it."

He didn't trouble to explain his qualifications, but had George Cassidy remembered that the great hall was hung with mirrors at short intervals, or had he taken the trouble on the night of the visitation to inspect the Napoleonic relics, he might have found an explanation for Manfred Cassidy's brain storm.

Chapter VI

The Red Chocolate

As I have beforetime remarked, the position of Private Clarence in the Sharpshooters was a unique one. That he, "a young man about town," should occupy the position of a private in His Majesty's Army, was not remarkable. The great war produced regiments which were filled with that peculiar phenomenon—the Nut in harness.

Private Clarence Cassidy's uniqueness lay in the fact that he had succeeded in raising the regiment in which he was now serving in so humble a capacity. For he had, as we know, suggested this great idea of drawing from other Line battalions their best shots—much to the disgust of the commanding officers of those battalions—and forming them into a separate and distinct corps under the somewhat bombastic and boastful title of the "Sharpshooters."

That at the beginning of the war Clarence Cassidy should find himself serving in a regiment in which three of his brothers held commissioned rank, was no freak of fate, but rather it was due to his own efforts and the power of that peculiar blarney which is the especial property of the man who is entitled to call himself a Cassidy.

So Clarence had, with fell design, secured the entry of his brethren into this excellent corps by the sheerest intrigue, and he had placed them in their several positions, one, George, as second-in-command; another, Manfred, commanding a company; and a third, Orlando, yet another company-commander, from sheer malice, because they had urged him to enlist, and had been foolish enough to suggest that he should confine his military activities to regiments with which they were not associated.

For the truth was that they stood in awe of their younger brother, whose bitter tongue and lamentable vocabulary of invective were a source of considerable distress to his relations. Then, when the war was at its height, and when the Sharpshooters, fighting an eternal rearguard action, justified the wisdom of their formation, Clarence had been oppressed with his lack of patriotism in securing for this fine corps three officers who, as he stated without consideration for anybody's feelings, and with no very great display of family pride, were wholly unworthy of the part which he had forced upon them.

And this he told them, heeding not their amour propre, and paying no regard to that paragraph of King's Regulations which lays down the attitude which a private soldier shall adopt towards his superior.

So Clarence openly stated his intention of ridding the regiment of those three officers, and it is a fact that two at least had gone. I have already related the circumstances of their disappearance. Orlando, addicted to postprandial weariness, had been taken prisoner when on reconnaissance duty. Manfred, the romantic, had seen the ghost of Napoleon, followed instantly by the martial apparition of the great Ney. And, though he had argued most strenuously with a speciously sympathetic medical officer, his case had been diagnosed as nerve strain, and he had been sent home to recuperate, to his intense disgust, for no sooner had he made a good recovery than he was most incontinently bagged for depot duty with the Wigshire Light Infantry. For in these days the War Office had no respect for the wishes of officers on leave, and would have as soon taken a rifleman and put him in command of a Highland regiment as not.

When the British Army was withdrawn from Soissons and rushed up to the north of France, and spread thinly even farther north along the banks of the Lys, the Sharpshooters was one of the first regiments to move and to be brought into operation. They were ordered, vaguely enough, to "make good the ground" north of a river which, even in their wildest geographical moments, they never dreamt had any existence, and to hold a trench line against the scattered units of the enemy, who, as we understand, had precisely the same instructions, only the other way about.

No man knew better the difficulties of the task assigned to them than Lieutenant-Colonel George Cassidy, who had received his promotion when his appointment to the command of the Sharpshooters had been confirmed. He sent for his younger brother before the regiment left its billets to march on its new front, and Private Cassidy came without the chaperonage which Regulations direct should be the lot of the private soldier when he confronts the majesty of commissioned rank.

George waited till Clarence closed the door behind him, then he got up from his chair.

"Mary Ann," he said, using the old family name which Clarence disliked, but which, nevertheless, he took a certain pleasure at this moment in hearing, "I've sent for you because we're going out on a pretty rotten job."

"And thinking I was a pretty rotter," suggested Clarence, "you wanted to tell me all about it."

George shook his head with a half smile. He opened his mouth to speak, but remained silent, his eyes gazing into space as one who was considering what was the best opening to a rather critical conversation. .

"The fact is, Mary Ann," said he, "a little time ago you suggested that Manfred Orlando and I ought to clear out of the regiment because we weren't quite good enough to associate with chaps like your nibs."

"Vulgarly put," said an admiring Clarence, "and as near the truth as makes no difference."

"H'm!" said George. "Well, Orlando disappeared and Manfred is gone, and I'm left. Now, what's your little scheme in regard to me? You see, Mary Ann, it's rather a serious business for me," he went on soberly, "because I'm commanding this regiment, and I want to keep all my wits about me for the next week or two."

"I think we'll call a truce till this affair is over," said Clarence, with a grin. "Really, George, you're not half a bad chap, and I've got ever so much more confidence in you than I had."

"You don't mean that, Mary Ann?" said his Colonel, with pathetic eagerness.

Clarence nodded solemnly.

"Yes. I think you're much smarter than people think you are," he said. "I'm getting quite a pleasant feeling about you. But"—he raised a warning finger—"don't get puffed up about this."

George Cassidy was not easily amused, save at a certain type of joke which blushes pinkly in a weekly journal; but here the humour of the situation seized him and he collapsed into his chair in a paroxysm of laughter.

"You always were a bully, Mary Ann," he said when he had exhausted himself. "Even as a kid you used to boss the whole house. But it is funny to realise that here am I, the Colonel of a regiment, taking my instructions meekly from a pup of a private."

"Are you trying to be offensive, George?" asked Private Cassidy severely.

"Get out!" said George, jerking his head at the door. "We march at dawn, but you needn't mention the fact. You're going to see some gory fighting, my son. If you ever live to wear a medal you're going to earn it."

Clarence stood at the door and gazed admiringly at his brother.

"You've been reading Old Moore's Almanack!" he accused. "And—what's that?"

George had taken a book out of the pocket of his overcoat. It was a peculiar book, if for no other reason because of its cover.

This was red—but a shade of red so bright and so brilliant as to be almost startling. It was a red that flamed vividly, turning all other reds to dinginess.

It was of a handy shape, something larger than a drill book and smaller than the conventional octavo of a novel.

"You'll have a copy to-night," said George. "The sergeant-major has one for every man of the battalion; in fact, the whole division is receiving a copy."

He placed the book in the outstretched hand of the other. On the cover in neat gold letters were the words:

"Trench Hints."

The cover was not the only remarkable feature.

"Why, it's chocolate!" said Clarence, conducting a rapid investigation.

"The best ever," chuckled George.

Chocolate it was, more carefully packed than any that Clarence, an authority upon confectionery, had ever seen. Tissue cover of red; foil cover of the same colour; and then, to ensure its safety, thin paper shavings—all of the same hue. The chocolate bore a label:

With the Compliments of

Harold Gosome,

of Newcastle.

"He's sent books to the gunners—they're blue—and books for the howitzer batteries—they're white," explained George. "He's a devil of a patriot, that young fellow!"

Clarence looked at the book thoughtfully, then he made his way to his billet to prepare for the coming trial.

No light trial was this, for which a little section of the British Army had prepared itself. Its task was to be immensely active and considerably offensive. The situation was best described in Clarence's own language.

"This jolly old regiment has got to make a noise like an Army Corps," said he, and that was pretty well the task which was allotted to the Sharpshooters.

For behind the screen it made long troop trains were running into small stations and disgorging thousands upon thousands of khaki-clad troops, and flat trucks stored with stained and weather-beaten guns; big horse-boxes, white-washed and littered, were turning out their reluctant passengers on to the sloping platforms; and in one small town, of which one had never heard till the war began, staff officers with their red-tabbed collars were as active as a hive of bees. Above circled a guardian aeroplane. Through the streets of the little town the cramped infantry stretched their legs with joyous freedom. Grimy cavalry passed in long streams through its crooked, narrow byways, and pottering asthmatic traction engines hauled guns of incredible size over its cobbled roadways. .

But whilst these gentlemen in khaki came at their leisure, the Sharpshooters and the Yorkshire regiment, with a regiment of rifles on their right, were making a noise not so much like an army corps as like an army itself. They dug trenches with furious haste; they submitted, in cold blooded inaction, to the sweeping rake of shrapnel and to the spraying fire of machine-guns; and all the time they were haunted with the knowledge that they neither knew where they were, nor exactly on what side they might expect to be attacked.

It was raining as it had rained ever since the Army came to Belgium. The ground over which the men marched to reach their fire trenches was a quagmire. The trenches were no sooner dug than they fell in, burying a struggling mass of swearing humanity which had to be rescued at some peril to the rescuer.

For a time it seemed that the enemy were content to play light with such a little force, but then one morning the German General Staff saw the danger and guessed the importance of the operations which were developing behind this frantic little screen. Against three battalions holding this forward line the enemy sent a division and a half of his best troops. Roughly speaking, in a division and a half there are 30,000 men, so that at the moment the odds against the front line were something like ten to one.

The German plan was obvious. It was to throw back the screen in disorder, unveil the enemy's weakness, and to strike swiftly a staggering blow at the disorganised—as he had judged it to be—mass of the detraining infantry, before it had time to form and deploy. It was a great scheme, and quite susceptible of execution, but for one important factor which the German General did not take into account.

That factor was the extraordinary density of the British soldier, who, having seen himself unquestionably enveloped on both flanks and outnumbered by a whole cloud of advancing Jaegers, yet nevertheless declined to accept the decision, violent as it was, as final. For when driven from his trenches by well-aimed shrapnel and by heavy gun fire, which crumbled the edge of the trenches and buried men alive so that they had to be dug out under a heavy fire, this British soldier again returned to the charge, and created for himself, on new and eccentric lines, new and more excellent trenches, firing back on the "victor" with such effect as to send him scurrying to the place from whence he came.

Clarence, crouched by the side of his brother, whose long-barrelled Browning rattled spasmodically, felt a sharp pain above his right eye and experienced a curious dampness all down one side of his face. He blinked back the blood, felt gingerly for the injury, and correctly diagnosed it as a flesh wound without complications. He whipped the little field-dressing from his inside pocket, and deftly fixed the bandage over his eye.

George looked round with a malicious little smile.

"Getting more and more like a wounded hero every day!" he said.

"Don't be disgusting," replied Clarence sternly.

The grey mass before them, swept back by rifle fire, had reformed. From the wood to the right came a new note of terror.

"Howitzers!" said George briefly. "Dig, you devils!"

And dig the Sharpshooters most assuredly did. Frantically, furiously, they struck down at the soft earth with their little spades and for all the world like a crowd of supers on a pantomime "trap" they began to sink deeper and deeper into the earth.

There followed a lull. Reinforcements were being hurried up. The boom of concealed howitzer batteries and the ceaseless crash of the British artillery brought a new note into the battle. The enemy was frankly bewildered. He expected to meet with little resistance, and had found himself driven back by an enemy which, he had been told, was numerically his inferior. The grey masses melted into their trenches, and a quarter of an hour after the battle had been at its height the field was bare of men, save the quiet figures which lay all along the British front.

Dusk came, and with it an order to improve the trench lines and to dig dummies; for, if there was one thing more necessary than another, it was to maintain the illusion that a strong force was holding the line.

Throughout the dark hours of the night, disturbed only by an occasional star shell, the brigade worked incessantly, concealing their own trench lines from the observer, turning the earth elsewhere to create spurious trench lines to invite the enemy's shelling, and planting before them rows of posts which from a distance would deceive the enemy into believing that they were protected by barbed-wire entanglements.

"We've got to hold on to the last man," said George, when he found a moment to speak in private to his brother. "Those are the Brigadier's orders, and apparently we can't possibly be reinforced for another three days."

Strangely enough, the attack next day was confined to artillery fire, and no attempt was made to shell the infantry. The British artillery were not so fortunate. The gunners' captain came up into the trenches for a closer view of his enemy.

"I can't understand it," he said. "As often as we shift our position the beggars discover us, though we cover the guns with grasses and the branches of trees."

"Their airmen," suggested George.

The other shook his head.

"It can't be that, though we've had their airmen over. We're too well concealed," he said. "Why, I've even got my men lying out as if they were infantry! And it's just the same with the howitzer people. The enemy's big guns have been shelling them all the morning, and their shells have been getting precious close."

For the rest of that day the artillery were more harassed than they had been for many months. No sooner did a battery shift its position than it was immediately located.

"They've got some system of signaling, I expect," said George, watching through his glasses the bursting shells.

Clarence, to whom he addressed his remark, started suddenly.

"Good Lord!" he gasped. And then: "I'd like you to let me go back, sir, along the communicating trench and try to reach the Brigadier," he said.

"What's the idea?" asked George curiously.

"If you'll allow me, I should like to go," insisted Clarence.

Five minutes later he was making the best of his way across a country raked by shell fire. He reached the Brigadier's headquarters and made his report, and two hours later was returning to the trench lines.

"You've been well out of it," said George. "The devils have been dropping shrapnel all over us, and I believe every regiment has been suffering the same."

"Did they shell the dummy trenches?"

"Not a bit," replied George gloomily. "We shall have to go out and improve those to-night. They wouldn't deceive a gas-pipe."

That evening Clarence made an extraordinary proposition to his commanding officer—a proposition which would have been violently rejected but for the fact that it was supported, a few minutes after the suggestion had been made, by a general order.

The next day, after the German aviators had come streaking across the trench lines, a heavy bombardment began from the German guns, and this time the shells were bursting with extraordinary accuracy over a line of trenches which contained nothing more important than a number of scattered little red books, placed in artistic disorder at regular intervals.

"I tumbled to it as soon as I saw the unnecessary inside packing to the chocolate," explained Clarence to his admiring brother. "I knew that that red had been chosen with great care, as it was not a usual colour. The inside wrappers, the shavings—all of the same vivid colour. Naturally our chaps would chuck the paper about. And the aviator, circling overhead, could always be pretty sure that in every trench one or two of these infernal red wrappers would be showing. That was how he found the artillery, and that was the way he spotted the howitzers—blue wrappers for one and white for the others. I should like to know who was the bright lad who thought out the scheme?"

There was a pause.

"You've done well out of it," said George, after a while.

He was obviously uncomfortable and avoided the steely suspicion in his brother's eyes.

"Fact is, old man," he blurted "the General asked me if I would recommend you for a commission and I said 'Yes.'"

The face of Clarence Cassidy fell.

"Dirty trick!" he hissed, and was genuinely upset.

Five Fateful Words

Sir George Farringdon was arrested on January 31st, and England was incoherent.

There had been fourteen days' delirium following the train robbery, and the arrest of the baronet was a tax upon the nation's sanity. Connoisseurs in crime had come post-haste to London. Haverson Judd, who specialised in 'hold-ups', came from New York: Russia sent M. Menshikoff: France sent Lebel. From every capital of Europe arrived some detective of note and standing: but it was Judd who unravelled the mystery to the intense annoyance of Andrews and his confrères at Scotland Yard. Yet the English police had made out an extraordinarily strong case against Farringdon; they had pieced the case together most cunningly. The story of the crime I need not relate at this stage. It will be sufficient to record a portion of the cross-examination. Though the trial is recorded in Ashton's Modern Cases, I am concerned less with the legal terminology of the indictment, or with the cited cases bearing upon the charge, than with the remarkable interruption by Mr. Haverson Judd of New York....

"Well?" There was triumph in the tone of the inquiry.

The English detective, with his broad, red face and his complacent smile, waited for the other's reluctant confession.

But the lean Yankee with the lazy eyes leant back and regarded his confrère through half-closed lids, an amused smile playing about the corners of his mouth.

"Well, sir?" he repeated. "What do you expect me to say?"

The Englishman grinned and jingled the coins in his pocket with perfect self-satisfaction.

"I expect you to admit that our methods, old fashioned as you think they are, take a lot of beating...."

"In fact," said Haverson Judd, languidly, "that the man who robbed the specie car of the Continental express was Sir George Farringdon?"

"Exactly:"

The American detective bit the end of a cigar and lit it at leisure.

"I reply 'No!'" he said, after a pause, "I've said 'No' all along, and I'm standing to it."

The Englishman jerked his shoulder impatiently.

"It was Jimmy the Dope," said Judd, calmly. "There's no crook raised on this side who could organise a hold-up of that description." There was a touch of pride in his voice. "The man must have been raised America, trained in America—"

"Huh!" Inspector Andrews could not refrain from this exhibition. "That's your confounded conceit."

They stood in the vestibule. Aimless witnesses shuffled to and fro nervously. Now and then there whisked past a flying gown of a barrister, bewigged and anxious.

A uniformed officer came towards them, "Farringdon's in the witness box."

Andrews whistled. "He's mad! His only chance lay in silence with Seton cross-examining. Come along, Judd."

Judd, smoking—contrary to every regulation—in the sacred precincts, dropped his cigar, crushed it under his heel, and followed.

At the door into the court he laid his hand on Andrews' arm.

"Jimmy the Dope," he said laconically. "This old cross-examination makes no difference to my decision."

A dull red bench ran the width of the court, and five solemn men sat listening. Under the great sword sat the Sherriff of the City. At the end of the row was an old, old man with a calm wise face.

His robes were of scarlet, a tightly-fitting wig covered his head; on his white hand was a ring with a great green stone. This was Mr Justice Grayham.

In the plain oak pulpit to his right stood the witness, tall, with weather-beaten face and steadfast grey eyes. A warder sat near him. Harold Seton, King's Counsel, his silk gown hitched forward over his shoulder, faced him in the well of the court. When the two men entered a clear voice was raised.

"Your life has been an adventurous one, Sir George?"

The witness smiled faintly. The warder who sat by the chair looked on with a responsive grin, as though he had a claim to a share of the adventure.

"I will take you back over your early career," said counsel. "You were born in India?"

"Yes."

"When you were four years of age your mother died?"

"Yes."

"Your father took entire control of you?"

"Yes."

"You had no nurse?"

"None."

"And even at that age you accompanied your father on his hunting trips?"

"Yes."

"He took charge of your education?"

"Yes."

"He was an eccentric man?"

"Yes, I suppose you would call him such."

"From India where did you go?"

"To Australia, South Africa, America."

"Your father was passionately fond of hunting?"

"Yes."

"And was killed by a lion in Somaliland?"

"Yes."

"How old were you then?"

"Ten, I think."

"Your father had a servant—a bodyguard, valet and companion—Simon Selby?"

"Yes."

"Who assumed charge of you from your father's death?"

"Yes."

"In terms of your father's will?"

"Yes: he was more than a servant—he was a friend of my father's."

"This Simon Selby, was he a well-educated man?"

"Yes; he spoke several languages."

"And you completed your education under his tuition?"

"Yes."

"You travelled all over the world. Did you come to England?"

"No, not till after Simon's death, seven years ago."

"You lived some time in the state of Washington?"

"Yes; and in Texas."

"Did you ever meet a man named Jimmy the Dope?"

The witness did not reply for a moment, then:

"Yes," he answered slowly.

"You first met him in Seattle?"

"Yes."

"He was a notoriously bad character—a train robber—was he not?"

"Yes."—more slowly.

"Did you shelter him for six months in your house outside Tacoma?"

"Yes; but I did not know who he was."

"Were not the newspapers filled with his exploits?"

"I believe they were."

"With full descriptions of him?"

"I believe so."

"And you did not realise that this guest of yours was a notorious criminal?"

"No."

The examining counsel bent his brows on the witness, but the gaze was returned.

"The sherriff of the court had heard that you had a strange guest, and wrote to you asking you to vouch for him?"

Again the witness hesitated.

"Yes, he did."

"And you did not reply?"

"No."

"Why not?"

The witness shrugged his shoulders.

"I believed the man when he told me his eyes had been injured, and he could not go abroad in daylight."

"But that does not answer my question. Why did you take no notice of the Sheriff's letter?"

"I don't know."

Counsel searched amongst the papers on the desk before him. Then:

"Were you a rich man?"

"There was plenty of money at home if I wanted it."

"That I know," said the lawyer, testily: "but for some reason or other you never drew upon the accumulated revenues of your English estate after Simon Selby's death. Had you plenty of money when Jimmy the Dope was your guest?"

Again the witness hesitated. "No," he said, at length.

The lawyer nodded, as though the reply had been in accordance with his information upon the subject.

"Now," he went on, "I am coming to the matter in relation to which you are charged. You returned to England three years ago?"

"Yes."

"And took up your residence at Farringdon Court?"

"Yes."

"You brought with you an American named Jonas E. Smyles?"

"Yes."

The lawyer paused: then he asked quietly:

"Smyles was dumb, was he not?"

The man in the box made no reply.

The question was repeated.

"Yes."

"I put it to you that you specially chose him because he was dumb?"

No reply.

"I suggest you took special pains to discover in Chicago a secretary who was deprived of human speech. Do you deny that?"

"No."

"What special reason had you?"

"I refuse to answer that question," the witness said, shortly.

The old judge leant forward and spoke gently.

"I think it would be wiser to answer; the jury are entitled to put an unfavourable construction upon your silence."

The witness bowed slightly.

"I had a secret to keep, my lord."

"What was that secret?" asked the barrister, sharply.

"I refuse to say."

"I suggest that you had been guilty of some act in America of which you were ashamed; that you dealt by correspondence with matters that you did not wish to be blazoned abroad?" accused counsel.

The man in the box shook his head.

"That is not so," he said simply.

"Your secretary is no longer with you?"

"No."

"He has not returned to America?"

"No."

"Do you know where he is?"

"Yes"—defiantly.

"Will you tell the Court?"

"No."

"I suggest," said the lawyer, "that you arranged for this man to keep out of the way?"

"That is so," admitted the other, calmly.

"To preserve your secret?"

The witness nodded, and a thrill ran through the crowded court.

The cross-examiner went on:

"On the night of January 17th this year the Kaiserin Gretchen called at Dover, and specie was landed to the value of £150,000. This was placed in a special train, which started at once for London. Between Langley and Tonbridge someone showed a red light, and the cars were brought to a stand-still. The train was boarded by two masked men, two of the bullion guards were shot, the treasure car was uncoupled, and the engine-driver was forced to proceed. When assistance was procured the robbers had disappeared, and the money. Now, Sir George, do you remember that night?"

"Yes."

"You have told us in your examination-in-chief that you had lent some man your motor car that afternoon?"

"Yes, I did."

"Was it the man who is known as Jimmy the Dope?"

"Yes." The answer came without hesitation.

"Will you tell us by what extraordinary process of reasoning you came to lend a convicted train-robber your car?"

The prisoner frowned a little.

"I tell you I did not know he was a thief."

"What!" The King's Counsel's voice was stern. "Do you tell us on your oath that you did not know the character of this man?"

"I do."

"Was not his conviction—subsequent to your entertaining him—public property in America?"

"I knew nothing about it," replied the witness, a little wearily.

"Will you swear that the Sherriff of Tacoma did not notify you of his arrest—that he did not inform you by telegram the day you arrived in New York from Tacoma that Jimmy the Dope had been arrested, and ask you to give evidence?"

There was no reply.

"I am going to prove," said counsel, addressing the jury, "that this telegram was received by the prisoner at Manhattan Hotel the day before he sailed for Europe. I am suggesting that he left the country sooner than give evidence against his friend. Now, sir, do you persist in saying you did not know the real character of Jimmy the Dope?"

"I still persist," said the witness, doggedly.

"I will not labour at a very obvious point," said counsel, dryly. "Well, this man, immediately after his release from jail, apparently set forth for England. He asked you to lend him your motor car—and you complied?"

"Yes. It was returned the next morning."

"In person?"

"No. It was found outside the lodge gates."

"Did you think that strange?"

"Yes; I thought it discourteous."

A titter of laughter followed his simple statement.

"If I tell you that your motor car was used to carry away the gold from the robbed car, will you accept that suggestion?"

"It is quite feasible," said the witness coolly.

"If I tell you that certain track marks corresponding with the tyres of your car have been traced, will you agree that the feasibility is a certainty?"

A shrug of the shoulder was the answer.

"Your home is thirty miles away from the scene of the robbery?"

"Yes."

"Are you aware how suspicion first fell upon you?"

"I am scarcely interested."

The witness reached his hand out for a glass of water as he made his reply.

"You are aware that the number of your car was recognised in the early hours of the following morning?"

"I am informed so."

"It was not actually traced until a fortnight later?"

"So I believe."

"It was a fortnight after the theft that you first made your statement concerning Jimmy the Dope?"

"Yes."

"For a fortnight you had been in possession of this knowledge—that a notorious train robber was in England; that he had been in your neighbourhood on the eve of the outrage—and yet you gave no information to the police?"

"Yes."

"Perhaps," said counsel, with biting sarcasm, "you had not heard of the robbery?"

"I had not."

Had a bomb exploded in court the sensation could not have been greater.

"You had not heard of a robbery that was the talk of the country?"

"That is so," confessed the man.

"Do you expect me to believe that?" thundered the lawyer.

The witness smiled.

"I'm afraid I expect you to believe very little that I say," he admitted ruefully.

"On your oath, you had not read about this extraordinary affair that filled columns of the daily Press?"

"I had not."

"Now, I want to ask you—" began the lawyer, but his junior plucked his gown; there was a whispered consultation.

Then he rose and faced the witness with a grave face.

"I wish to impress upon you the seriousness of the questions I am putting to you," he said, quietly. "I have been informed that on the day following the robbery a full account of the affair was sent you by the chief constable of the county, in the hope that you, as a motorist, might be able to help trace the motor car; this letter was delivered to you. Do you still deny that you had learnt nothing of the robbery?"

The man gripped the ledge of the box before him, and the bulldog thrust of his under-jaw betrayed something of his emotions.

"I absolutely deny any knowledge," he said, loudly.

Again he met the challenge of the lawyer's eyes unflinchingly.

"When you were arrested," counsel resumed, "A search was made in your house?"

"Yes."

"Do you know," the lawyer spoke deliberately—"that twelve thousand pounds in gold were found?"

"Yes."

"In gold—in specie?"

"Yes. I always keep large quantities of gold in the house."

"Why?"

"For expenses."

"But you have a bank?"

"I have not employed the bank since—"

"Ah!"

The examiner's finger pointed at him.

"Since Jonas Smyles left you for his holiday?"

The witness drew a long breath.

"Yes, since Jonas left."

"Since the custodian of your secret went away—taking his holiday at an opportune moment?"

Something amused the witness, for he smiled.

"The holiday was a genuine one," he said. "It coincided with this unfortunate affair."

"When you were arrested did you see the reporter of the Megaphone?"

"He saw me."

"Did he ask you to make a statement for his paper?"

"Yes." The eyes of the witness twinkled. "I said, 'My statement to you is this—Jonas must not return!"

"An extraordinary thing to say, was it not?"

"It was a brilliant idea," said the witness, coolly, "for my message was printed in the paper."

"A brilliant idea, indeed!" said the lawyer, with a touch of irony.

"Now," he continued, "I should like to ask you to inform the Court what explanation you can give to the presence of this huge sum of money in your home?"

"I have given the explanation."

"That it was for current expenses?"

"Yes."

"From what bank was it drawn?"

"A London bank?"

"Which London bank?"

"I refuse to state."

"And you expect us to believe that?"

"No."

"I suggest that it formed part of the proceeds of the robbery?"

"A contemptible suggestion," said the witness, showing sign of impatience—the first he had shown. "Why should I steal money? Why should I who have more money than I need, rob a bullion car?"

The two detectives heard, the one with growing satisfaction, the American with knit brows. It was when the lawyer had done with his next question that Mr Haverson Judd outraged the frigid propriety of an English court.

"I cannot answer why you should have done this. It is not for me to hazard an opinion," the lawyer was saying, "There are men who break the law out of sheer perversity, who rob because there is some unnatural kink in them. I would really rather you reconciled these statements of yours—how you came to harbour this train robber in America, why you swear you knew nothing of his character, what reason you have for saying you knew nothing of the train robbery, why you employed a dumb secretary, and stored huge sums of gold—"

"Stop, sir!"

It was the American, his eyes blazing with excitement, who sprang to his feet.

"I can answer you!" he cried, and spoke five words:

They overlooked the breach of court etiquette.

No man called for silence. Judge, jury, lawyers, ushers, sat momentarily paralysed by the tense phrase, and the prisoner, with flushed face, nodded slowly to the judge.

"Yes, your lordship, that is true," he faltered. "I have been a vain fool to hide it—that is the explanation."

The judge was skimming his notes. He finished and nodded.

"Very remarkable," he said. "There can be little doubt that the case for the prosecution has collapsed."

"Of course it explains everything," said Judd, later. "Explains Jimmy the Dope—did I tell you the Liverpool police caught him this morning?—and why Farringdon kept the money by him, drawing it in bulk from the bank, and why he swore he knew nothing of the robbery. It explains Simon Selby, too, and why Farringdon, with his huge estates in England, was a poor man in America. But wasn't it extraordinary that I didn't get wise to the solution until the prosecution used that curious sentence, 'really rather you reconciled.' Do you see the connection?"

Richard Horatio Edgar Wallace was born on the 1st April 1875 at 7 Ashburnham Grove, Greenwich. His mother, Mary Jane "Polly" Richards was born into an Irish Catholic family in Liverpool in 1843 and had worked in theatres, both as an actress in bit-parts and as a stagehand and usherette, until she married a Merchant Navy Captain, Joseph Richards, in 1867. He too had been born into an Irish Catholic family in Liverpool. His father had also been a Captain in the Merchant Navy, and his mother's family had a marine background. Mary was eight months pregnant with Joseph's child when he died at sea, and it was once the child had been born that she first turned to the stage, taking the stage name Polly Richards.

She joined the Marriott family theatre troupe in 1872. It was managed by Mrs. Alice Edgar, Richard Edgar, Grace Edgar, Adeline Edgar and Richard Horatio Edgar, Wallace's father. In late 1874 Mary and Richard Horatio Edgar had a brief sexual encounter at the party following a successful show, and she fell pregnant. Worried about the scandal which would ensue and fearing that she might forever lose her job at the troupe, she fabricated an obligation in Greenwich would detain her there for at least six months. She lived in a room in the boarding house on Ashburnham Grove until her son, Edgar, was born. She had already made preparations through her midwife for a couple to foster the child, and when Edgar was born the midwife presented her with Mrs Freeman. Her husband was a fishmonger at Billingsgate market and she already had ten children. She was happy to foster the child and for Polly to make frequent visits to see him in exchange for a small sum of money which Polly made from her work in the theatre troupe.

Wallace was now known as Richard Horatio Edgar Freeman, taking his father's forenames and his foster family's surname. Broadly speaking his childhood was a happy one. The Freemans looked after him lovingly and he had good friendships with his foster siblings, particularly Clara Freeman, twenty years his senior, who often looked after him as a child. After a few years Polly's finances tightened and she was no longer in a position to afford the fee she had been paying the Freemans. However, they had grown to love the young Wallace and opted to adopt him in order to keep him out of the workhouse. Polly could no longer visit him. George Freeman was keen to ensure that he had equal opportunities and did all he could to secure him an education at St. Alfege with St. Peter's, a Peckham boarding school. Despite his adoptive father's efforts, though, Wallace left the school aged twelve for truancy.

Instead he went to work and by the time he was fourteen or fifteen he had experience selling newspapers at Ludgate Circus, near Fleet Street, as a worker in a rubber factory, as a shoe shop assistant, as a milk delivery boy and as a ship's cook. He stole from the milk company which resulted in his dismissal, and in 1894 was engaged to a local girl from Deptford named Edith Anstree, though he broke this off and instead joined the Infantry. He adopted the name Edgar Wallace which he took from Lew Wallace, the author of *Ben-Hur*, and his medical record records a diminutive 33" chest and a stunted growth. his first posting was with the West Kent Regiment in South Africa in 1896, though he did not enjoy military life, arranging to be transferred to the Royal Army Medical Corps. Though this was a less strenuous job, it was also significantly less pleasant and so he again transferred to the Press Corps, which he found suited him far better.

He was in Cape Town in 1898 where he met Rudyard Kipling and was inspired to begin writing and publishing poetry and songs. His first collection of ballads, *The Mission that Failed!* and was enough of a success that in 1899 he paid his way out of the armed forces in order to turn to writing full time. His first work was as a war correspondent for Reuters who kept him in Africa to cover the Boer War, and then for the Daily Mail in 1900 and various other periodicals after that. It was while he was in South Africa that he met and married Ivy Maude Caldecott, who was 21 when they married in 1901, despite her Wesleyan missionary father's strong opposition to the union, for several reasons, one of which was that Wallace's writing was not turning quite the profit he had expected it would. *War and Other Poems* and *Writ in Barracks*, both published in 1900, had not proved as popular as his first collection. Eleanor Clare Hellier Wallace, their first child, died of meningitis in 1903 and, in rather deep debt, they returned to London. Wallace used his contacts with the Daily Mail to get work with them in London, electing to write detective novels as a means of making quick money.

Wallace met Polly, his birth mother, in 1903. He didn't remember her from his childhood as he had been too young when she became unable to visit, so it was as though they were meeting for the first time. She was sixty years old and terminally ill, living in abject poverty. She had come to Wallace seeking financial support, but he turned her away. She died in the Bradford Infirmary later that year. In 1904 he and Ivy had a son, Bryan. He was still writing and had completed his first thriller, *The Four Just Men*. Since nobody would publish it he resorted to setting up his own publishing company which he called Tallis Press and he published a serialised version of *The Four Just Men* in 1905. He received promotional assistance from the Daily Mail in which he ran a competition for entrants to guess the method of murder in the final chapter, with a prize of £1,000 for a correct guess. Although the paper's proprietor, Lord Alfred Harmsworth, refused Wallace the £1,000 prize money, Wallace persisted and went ahead with the competition, recklessly advertising on billboards and buses all over the country, hoping to expand his advertisements across the Empire. His worried colleagues at the Daily Mail managed to convince him to lower the prize money to £500, split into a first prize of £250, a second prize of £200 and a third of £50, but with the total cost of his advertisements nearing £2,000 he would need to sell £2,500 worth of copies before he could see any profit. He was confident that this could be achieved in just three months.

Though he had remarkable enthusiasm, it became clear that his managerial skills left a lot to be desired. It soon emerged that nowhere in the competition terms and conditions had he included a clause limiting the competition to one single winner; instead, any entrant with a winning answer was entitled to their corresponding prize money. Thus, if ten entrants guessed the first prize answer, the competition was obliged to pay each entrant £250. This error was only noticed after the competition had been closed and the solution had been printed in the final installment of the novel, meaning that not only was there no opportunity to write his way out of enormous financial obligation, but the entrants who had guessed correctly would by now have read the final chapter and know they had done so. £250 was an enormous amount of money to the average Edwardian family and those entitled to it were likely to make a lot of noise if they didn't receive their money. Despite this, Wallace's fist instinct was to attempt to ignore the issue entirely, even as he discovered that he initial calculations had been dramatically over-enthusiastic and it would take nearer to two years of continuous sales to break even at the initial cost of £2,500, let alone the new figure which included every correct guesser. Compounding the problem even further was the awful realisation that as sales continued throughout the initial three month period and Wallace approached the £2,500 break-even figure, new readers were still eligible to enter and guess correctly. Though it is unknown how much he eventually owed his readers, Lord Harmsworth found himself having to loan over £5,000 in order to protect the reputation of the newspaper, since 1906 had come around and there still hadn't been a list printed of all prize-winners. It was less a charitable act than one of a man anxious that the failure would reflect ill on his own paper. Wallace filed for bankruptcy shortly thereafter and as a token gesture to his creditors sold the rights to the novel to Sir George Newnes, a publisher and editor, for £75. In the midst of this chaos though, Wallace managed to write and published *Smithy*, which would become the first of a series of *Smithy* novels.

Following this fiascos Wallace was dismissed from the Daily Mail in 1907 when inaccuracies which were found in his reporting, resulting in libel cases being brought against the paper. That year he became the first reporter to be fired from the Daily Mail and was his awful reputation prevented him from finding work at any other papers. Despite all this, though, he travelled to the Congo Free State later that year and reported on the criminal treatment of the Congolese people by King Leopold II of Belgium and the Belgian rubber companies. Up to fifteen million Congolese were killed in various atrocities, and Wallace was asked to serialise stories based on his experiences for her penny magazine *Weekly Tale-Teller*. He and Ivy had another daughter, named Patricia, in 1908. Though his new work for *Weekly Tale-Teller* was bringing in some money, their financial situation was still dire and Ivy was occasionally forced to sell off her jewellery and possessions in order to pay for food. In 1911 his Congolese stories were published in a collection called *Sanders of the River*, which quickly became a bestseller. He would publish eleven more such collections featuring a total of 102 stories of adventure and tribal life set on the river Congo.

From 1908 he started to enjoy a revival of both his success and his reputation. The majority of his initial writing he sold outright in order to make money as quickly as possible and placate his creditors in the United Kingdom and South Africa, but as his success saw the reestablishment of his reputation he began to find work once again as a journalist, beginning in horse racing for the *Week-End*, the *Evening News* and then as an editor for the *Week-End Racing Supplement*. Following this success he started his own racing papers, *Bibury's* and *R. E. Walton's Weekly*, eventually buying his own racehorses and losing thousands gambling. His success was insufficient to support his newly extravagant lifestyle and his marriage began to fail in the light of his financial irresponsibility. He and Ivy had their last child together, Michael Blair Wallace, in 1916, and she filed for divorce in 1918 moving to Tunbridge Wells with her children.

Wallace began to fall for his secretary Ethel Violet King and they married in 1921, having a child, Penelope Wallace, in 1923, who would herself go on to become a successful crime writer. Wallace now began to take his career as a fiction writer more seriously, signing with Hodder and Stoughton in 1921. He now began to organize his contracts more carefully, arranging for royalties and properly organized promotions, run by people more business-minded than himself. He was marketed as the 'King of Thrillers' and they gave him the trademark image of a trilby, a cigarette holder and a yellow Rolls Royce. He was truly prolific, capable not only of producing a 70,000 word novel in three days but of doing three novels in a row in such a manner. His publishers signed off on almost everything he wrote as soon as he turned it in, estimating that by 1928 one in four books being read at any time was written by Wallace, for alongside his famous thrillers he wrote variously in other genres, including but not limited to science fiction, non-fiction accounts of WWI which amounted to ten volumes and screen plays. Eventually he would reach the remarkable total of 170 novels, 18 stage plays and 957 short stories.

Wallace became chairman of the Press Club which to this day holds an annual Edgar Wallace Award, rewarding 'excellence in writing'. In 1923 he broadcasted a report on the Epsom Derby horse race for the British Broadcasting Company, making him the first ever radio sports correspondent. His ex-wife Ivy had suffered from breast cancer between 1923-1924, and it eventually killed her in 1926 despite a successful operation to remove a tumour the year before. He wrote the essay "The Canker in our Midst" in 1926 which dealt, aggressively and controversially, with the problem of paedophilia in show business, describing how children were unwittingly left open to sexual abuse, and linking paedophilia with homosexuality. Its tone has been described as "intolerant, blustering, kick-the-blighters-down-the-stairs". He was appointed chairman of the British Lion Film Corporation on the back of the success of *The Ringer* and on the agreement that he give British Lion first choice on all his future work. This contract gave him an annual salary and a large amount of stock with the company, along with a stipend on all British Lion production of his work and 10% of their annual profits. This extraordinary contract gave him annual earnings by 1929 of almost £50,000, or almost £2 million in 2014.

He now became an active figure in politics, entering the 1931 general election as a Liberal contestant in Blackpool, rejecting the current government in favour of free trade. He lost the election by over 33,000 votes and went to America in late 1931, once again deeply in debt after buying the *Sunday News* which closed six months later. In America he quickly found work as a script doctor for RKO Pictures, enjoying early success with the 1932 adaptation of *The Hound of the Baskervilles*. This success, along with that of the play *The Green Pack*, established his reputation in America and he was able to see his own work adapted for film, beginning with *The Four Just Men*. His most successful theatrical work, *On The Spot*, which explores the life of Al Capone, has been described as "arguably, in construction, dialogue, action, plot and resolution, still one of the finest and purest of 20th-century melodramas". These successes led to his assignation on RKO's "gorilla picture" which would become famous as King Kong in 1933.

He worked on the first draft though he was beginning to experience severe headaches which brought about a diagnosis of diabetes. Despite taking medication to address his condition, it deteriorated in a matter of days. His wife booked him passage home but soon heard that he had entered a coma and died of his condition and double pneumonia on the 7th of February 1932 in North Maple Drive, Beverly Hills. In his honour the bell at St. Bride's church on Fleet Street tolled for the duration of the morning while the flags flew at half-mast. He was buried near his home in England at Chalklands, Bourne End, in Buckinghamshire. Once again, at the time of his death he was in severe debt, mostly to racing bookkeepers, though these debts were settled within two years thanks to the enormous royalties his estate continued to receive from his contracts. His writing has been translated into 29 languages, and is considered one of the most important bodies of Colonial writing.

Edgar Wallace – A Concise Bibliography

African Novels
Sanders of the River (1911)
The People of the River (1911)
The River of Stars (1913)
Bosambo of the River (1914)
Bones (1915)
The Keepers of the King's Peace (1917)
Lieutenant Bones (1918)
Bones in London (1921)
Sandi the Kingmaker (1922)
Bones of the River (1923)
Sanders (1926)
Again Sanders (1928)

Four Just Men (Series)
The Four Just Men (1905)
The Council of Justice (1908)
The Just Men of Cordova (1917)
The Law of the Four Just Men (US title: Again the Three Just Men) (1921)
The Three Just Men (1926)

Again the Three Just Men (US title: The Law of the Three Just Men) (1929) a.k.a. Again the Three

Mr. J. G. Reeder (Series)
Room 13 (1924)
The Mind of Mr. J. G. Reeder (US title: The Murder Book of Mr. J. G. Reeder) (1925)
Terror Keep (1927)
Red Aces (1929)
The Guv'nor and Other Short Stories (US title: Mr. Reeder Returns) (1932)

Detective Sgt. (Inspector) Elk series
The Nine Bears or The Other Man or The Cheaters (1910)
revised as Silinski - Master Criminal (1930)
The Fellowship of the Frog (1925)
The Joker or The Colossus (1926)
The Twister (1928)
The India-Rubber Men (1929)
White Face (1930)

Educated Evans (Series)
Educated Evans (1924)
More Educated Evans (1926)
Good Evans (1927)

Smithy (Series)
Smithy (1905)
Smithy Abroad (1909)
Smithy and The Hun (1915)
Nobby or Smithy's Friend Nobby (1916)

Crime Novels
Angel Esquire (1908)
The Fourth Plague or Red Hand (1913)
Grey Timothy or Pallard the Punter (1913)
The Man Who Bought London (1915)
The Melody of Death (1915)
A Debt Discharged (1916)
The Tomb of T'Sin (1916)
The Secret House (1917)
The Clue of the Twisted Candle (1918)
Down under Donovan (1918)
The Man Who Knew (1918)
The Strange Lapses of Larry Loman (1918)
The Green Rust (1919)
Kate Plus Ten (1919)
The Daffodil Mystery or The Daffodil Murder (1920)
Jack O' Judgment (1920)
The Angel of Terror or The Destroying Angel (1922)
The Crimson Circle (1922)

Mr. Justice Maxwell or Take-A-Chance Anderson (1922)
The Valley of Ghosts (1922)
Captains of Souls (1923)
The Clue of the New Pin (1923)
The Green Archer (1923)
The Missing Million (1923)
The Dark Eyes of London or The Croakers (1924)
Double Dan or Diana of Kara-Kara (US Title) (1924)
The Face in the Night or The Diamond Men or The Ragged Princess (1924)
The Sinister Man (1924)
The Three Oak Mystery (1924)
The Blue Hand or Beyond Recall (1925)
The Daughters of the Night (1925)
The Gaunt Stranger or Police Work (1925) revised as The Ringer (1926)
A King by Night (1925)
The Strange Countess (1925)
The Avenger or The Hairy Arm (1926)
The Black Abbot (1926)
The Day of Uniting (1926)
The Door with Seven Locks (1926)
The Man from Morocco or Souls In Shadows or The Black (US Title) (1926)
The Million Dollar Story (1926)
The Northing Tramp or The Tramp (1926)
Penelope of the Polyantha (1926)
The Square Emerald or The Woman (1926)
The Terrible People or The Gallows' Hand (1926)
We Shall See! or The Gaol-Breakers (US Title) (1926)
The Yellow Snake or The Black Tenth (1926)
Big Foot (1927)
The Feathered Serpent or Inspector Wade or Inspector Wade and the Feathered Serpent (1927)
Flat 2 (1927)
The Forger or The Counterfeiter (1927)
Terror Keep (1927)
The Hand of Power or The Proud Sons of Ragusa (1927)
The Man Who Was Nobody (1927)
Number Six (1927)
The Squeaker or The Sign of the Leopard or The Squealer (US Title) (1927)
The Traitor's Gate (1927)
The Double (1928)
The Flying Squad (1928)
The Gunner or Gunman's Bluff (US Title) (1928)
Four Square Jane or The Fourth Square (1929)
The Golden Hades or Stamped In Gold or The Sinister Yellow Sign (1929)
The Green Ribbon (1929)
The Calendar (1930)
The Clue of the Silver Key or The Silver Key (1930)
The Lady of Ascot (1930)
The Devil Man or Sinister Street or Silver Steel

or The Life and Death of Charles Peace (1931)
The Man at the Carlton or The Mystery of Mary Grier (1931)
The Coat of Arms or The Arranways Mystery (1931)
On the Spot: Violence and Murder in Chicago (1931)
When the Gangs Came to London or Scotland Yard's Yankee Dick
or The Gangsters Come To London (1932)
The Frightened Lady or The Case of the Frightened Lady or Criminal At Large (1933)
The Green Pack (1933)
The Man Who Changed His Name (1935)
The Mouthpiece (1935)
Smoky Cell (1935)
The Table (1936)
Sanctuary Island (1936)

Other Novels
Captain Tatham of Tatham Island or Eve's Island or The Island of Galloping Gold (1909)
The Duke in the Suburbs (1909)
Private Selby (1912)
1925 - The Story of a Fatal Peace (1915)
Those Folk of Bulboro (1918)
The Book of all Power (1921)
Flying Fifty-five (1922)
The Books of Bart (1923)
Barbara on Her Own (1926)

Poetry Collections
The Mission That Failed (1898)
War and Other Poems (1900)
Writ In Barracks (1900)

Non-Fiction
Unofficial Despatches of the Anglo-Boer War (1901)
Famous Scottish Regiments (1914)
Field Marshal Sir John French (1914)
Heroes All: Gallant Deeds of the War (1914)
The Standard History of the War – Volumes 1 – 4 (1914)
Kitchener's Army and the Territorial Forces:
The Full Story of a Great Achievement (1915)
Vol. 2-4. War of the Nations (1915)
Vol. 5-7. War of the Nations (1916)
Vol. 8-9. War of the Nations (1917)
Famous Men and Battles of the British Empire (1917)
Tam of the Scouts (1918)
The Real Shell-Man: The Story of Chetwynd of Chilwell (1919)
People or Edgar Wallace by Himself (1926)
The Trial of Patrick Herbert Mahon (1928)
My Hollywood Diary (1932)

Screenplays

King Kong (1932, first draft of original screenplay, 110 pages) While the script was not used in its entirety, much of it was retained for the final screenplay.
The Hound of the Baskervilles (1932, British film)
The Squeaker (1930, British film)
Prince Gabby (1929, British film)
Mark of the Frog (1928, American film)
The Valley of Ghosts (192

Short Story Collections

The Admirable Carfew (1914)
The Adventure of Heine (1917)
Tam O' the Scouts (1918)
The Fighting Scouts (1919)
Chick (1923)
The Black Avons (1925)
The Brigand (1927)
The Mixer (1927)
This England (1927)
The Orator (1928)
The Thief in the Night (1928)
Elegant Edward (1928)
The Lone House Mystery and Other Stories (1929)
The Governor of Chi-Foo (1929)
Again the Ringer The Ringer Returns (US Title) (1929)
The Big Four or Crooks of Society (1929)
The Black or Blackmailers I Have Foiled (1929)
The Cat-Burglar (1929)
Circumstantial Evidence (1929)
Fighting Snub Reilly (1929)
For Information Received (1929)
Forty-Eight Short Stories (1929)
Planetoid 127 and The Sweizer Pump (1929)
The Ghost of Down Hill & The Queen of Sheba's Belt (1929)
The Iron Grip (1929)
The Lady of Little Hell (1929)
The Little Green Man (1929)
The Prison-Breakers (1929)
The Reporter (1929)
Killer Kay (1930)
Mrs William Jones and Bill (1930)
Forty Eight Short Stories (George Newnes Limited ca. 1930)
The Stretelli Case and Other Mystery Stories (1930)
The Terror (1930)
The Lady Called Nita (1930)
Sergeant Sir Peter or Sergeant Dunn, C.I.D. (1932)
The Scotland Yard Book of Edgar Wallace (1932)
The Steward (1932)

Nig-Nog and other humorous stories (1934)
The Last Adventure (1934)
The Woman From the East (1934) Co-written By Robert George Curtis
The Edgar Wallace Reader of Mystery and Adventure (1943)
The Undisclosed Client (1963)

Other

King Kong, with Draycott M. Dell, (1933), 28 October 1933 Cinema Weekly

Plays

An African Millionaire (1904)
The Forest of Happy Dreams (1910)
Dolly Cutting Herself (1911)
The Manager's Dream (1914)
M'Lady (1921)
Double Dan (1926)
The Mystery of room 45 (1926)
A Perfect Gentleman (1927)
The Terror (1927)
Traitors Gate (1927)
The Lad (1928)
The Man Who Changed His Name (1928)
The Squeaker (1928)
The Calendar (1929)
Persons Unknown (1929)
The Ringer (1929)
The Mouthpiece (1930)
On the Spot (1930)
Smoky Cell (1930)
The Squeaker (1930)
To Oblige A Lady (1930)
The Case of the Frightened Lady (1931)
The Old Man (1931)
The Green Pack (1932)
The Table (1932)

www.ingramcontent.com/pod-product-compliance
Lightning Source LLC
Chambersburg PA
CBHW072001170626
46813CB00005B/1966